THE
CHAMELEON

A NOVEL

Matt Micros

For the chameleon in us all...

TABLE OF CONTENTS

THE CHAMELEON

"We are like chameleons, we take our hue and the color of our moral character, from those who are around us."

John Locke

I
~THE BET~

In a world of pushing, shoving, striving-to-get-ahead at all costs people; to those who knew him well, John Mann was a breath of fresh air. His father, however, had always had a differing assessment of him that usually involved a few expletives sandwiched around the four-letter word, "lazy". When his friends described him as the smartest person they knew, his father referred to him as an "enormous waste of god-given ability". The truth, as is usually the case in life, probably lay somewhere in between the two descriptions, although I tended to side more closely with his friends' version; mostly because I was one.

Neighbors since birth, friends shortly thereafter, and classmates since Kindergarten, John and I starred together on our high school football and basketball teams, and starred separately on the baseball and golf teams respectively. We were more complements than competitors. If John had a competitor, he came in the form of a self-motivated, egocentric, intellectual named Alan Huber. I say "if" because in order to have a competition, there needed to be at least two people competing, but John had no interest in that, which is why he split nearly every award and honor in the school with Alan, instead of hoarding them all to himself. John was number one in the class academically. Alan was number two. (I was 97th in case you were curious.) John was President of the Varsity Club. Alan was Student Body President. After graduation, Alan went off to study Pre-Law at Harvard. John went off to play football at Yale. Four years later, Alan graduated as the valedictorian of his class, while John graduated as a two-time All-American and the school's all-time leading rusher.

That was where they took two decidedly divergent paths, and where John's father began to develop his rather harsh opinion of him. Alan eventually became the youngest State's Attorney in Connecticut history. Meanwhile, John moved to California and managed a bar in a comfortable little beach town south of Los Angeles, becoming the owner when the original owner passed away and left it to him in his will. It was at that point that John and I were reunited after a six year separation, and without meaning to pat myself on the back too heartily, I am convinced that if we hadn't been, he would have continued to drift through a life of relative obscurity, succeeding only when success came easily to him—something that was happening less and less frequently as he grew older.

It was twilight by the time I finished the 15 minute ride from LAX to Hermosa Beach, and dozens of volleyball players scrambled to finish their matches before dark. Hundreds of people were also walking along the Strand—the 25 mile bike and walking path that connected Redondo Beach to Malibu—some to relax after a long day at work, others to continue what had already been a relaxing day.

Facing the clear blue ocean a mere few feet from the sandy courts of pro beach volleyball's most prestigious tournament, *The Shanty* was the definition of a dive beach bar. No matter how many times John had described it to me over the phone, I always felt as though he was exaggerating its deficiencies—until I stepped into the place for the first time. It had tall, well-worn oak tables and stools both inside and on the covered patio outside. Stains and carvings on them were more the norm than the exception, as if it was encouraged, and more sand was visible on the floor than hardwood. The sign above the entrance read, "NO SHIRT, NO SHOES, NO PROBLEM". The typical crowd in the bar was one of the more eclectic and diverse ones around. There were the local barflies bellied up to one end of the bar, while a few shirtless pro beach volleyball players shared a pitcher at the other end. A collection of wannabe actors and actresses convened at a large table in the middle of the room, arguing over the merits of the newest batch of television shows they were not a part of. In the far corner, an actual successful actor who was only in *The Shanty* so he could spend a night in relative anonymity, sat with two friends. Also in the bar at 6:00pm on your typical Tuesday night in November, were three of the most stunning women I had ever laid eyes on. Their six foot statures and bikini bottoms indicated that they had just stepped in for a drink from the volleyball courts. Most of the men in the bar were far too intimidated to even speak to them. Either that, or they were realistic enough to know that these women were clearly out of their league. But there was always *one* guy with unwarranted confidence. A good looking guy, who had been a great looking guy a few years back, but hadn't yet come to terms with the fact that he wasn't twenty-five anymore. Steve Abbott was now thirty-something, and carrying a few extra pounds on a frame that was topped off with a tussle of dark hair. He got up from the table of wannabes and marched over to the young ladies in question.

"You know what would look good on you?" he asked one of them.

She cringed at the response she knew was coming.

"Me," he continued.

She rolled her eyes and looked away. Undaunted, Abbott turned to one of her friends as if she was part of a to-do list. "That's a great bikini. I bet it would look even better crumpled up next to my bed in the morning."

"Weak," the girl responded.

He turned to the third one. "So how about a pizza and a fuck?"

With no hesitation, she slapped him across the face with the force of a Serena Williams forehand, before all three walked away.

"What?!" he yelled after her, "you don't like pizza?! We can eat something else!"

With his easy smile, Hawaiian shirt, cargo shorts and Banana Republic flip flops, the man behind the bar looked even more relaxed and casual than I had remembered him, "Could you try not to chase off all the women in the place?" John Mann said.

"I don't see any women in here," Abbott responded, looking around.

"Not anymore," John laughed before he noticed me standing ten feet away. "Holy crap," he continued as he hurdled the bar with the ease of a pommel horse medalist. "As I live and breathe. Nick Lawson. What are *you* doing here?!"

"I got tired of the snow and cold weather," I answered.

"Are you visiting or moving here?"

"Moved."

"Do you have a job?"

"Nope. But from what I can see, no one seems to work much out here anyway."

"Do you need a place to stay?"

"Nope."

"Where are you staying?"

"With you," I said matter-of-factly.

"What makes you think that's an option?" he smiled.

"Because you need me out here."

"And why is that?"

"Because someone has to prevent you from throwing yourself into the Pacific."

"Now why would I do that?"

I pointed at the television.

"It's all over in Connecticut," Fox News Anchor, Megyn Kelly said, "as a Democrat has been elected the youngest Governor in United States history. At thirty-three years and seven months, Alan Huber has defeated Ron Baldelli by a margin of 52 to 48 percent."

"I'm happy for him," John replied, feigning indifference.

"Huber was John's biggest rival in high school," I explained to the men seated at the bar. "They were number one and two in the class academically. John was number one. Huber was Student Body President. John was President of the Varsity Club. Huber went to Harvard. John went to Yale—"

The older of the two men at the bar interjected, "And now he's a Governor and John's a bartender."

"I'm not just a bartender. I'm the owner," John answered.

"You own this shithole? I always thought you were just helping out a friend to pick up a little cash."

"If this place is such a shithole, how come you're in here all day, every day?"

"Because I can't afford to go to a nice place."

"Fair enough," John laughed. "And no matter what you guys all think, I wish Alan well."

"A tale of two lives," I said. "Does it ever bother you that you've failed to do more with the abilities God gave you?"

"You sound like my father."

I always had been good at pushing John's buttons.

"I'm here because I want to be here," he continued. "I like my life. I don't ever have to put on a suit and tie except for weddings and funerals. I make an ok living meeting colorful people. I don't have anyone to tie me down. I'm a lone wolf. Howling at the moon."

"You're here because you can't work for anyone else. You've either been fired or walked off of every other job you've had. And if by *ok living meeting colorful people*, you mean hanging out with drunks and bar flies, while making slightly above minimum wage, then yes, I agree. And you don't have anyone to tie you down because you have serious commitment issues. As for that lone wolf thing.... I'll give you that one," I answered.

"That Huber guy must have a lot going for him. He'll probably be President some day," the older man at the bar offered.

Abbott was smiling behind John. He knew they had him going now.

"Oh, he's had plenty going for him," John began. "He got into Harvard because his father built the library. He got into Harvard Law because his uncle went to college with the Dean. And after dating the Dean's ugly daughter for four years, the Dean then got him the job in the State Attorney's Office. As for the election, his family had 100 times more money than the other candidate."

"So you're saying the only reason he's successful, is because of the advantages he's had?" I asked.

"I'm saying that *anyone* with his advantages would be Governor right now."

"Interesting," Abbott said. "I smell a bet coming on."

"What kind of bet?" John inquired.

I thought it over. "So you think with certain advantages, you could do anything and be successful?"

"Anything within reason."

"Ok. I'm just free-flowing ideas here, but how bout this. We pick ten occupations. From that list, you have to choose five of them. You'll have a maximum of six months to succeed at each. We'll give you every advantage you need to help you get the jobs."

"What kind of advantages can you guys give me?" John asked skeptically.

"I know a lot of people," Abbott said.

"I'm not sure I want to know the people you know."

"I'm serious. Anything goes," I told him. "You can lie on your resume. Cheat. Beg. Borrow. Steal. Call in favors. Whatever you need to do to get the job. After that, it will be performance based."

"What kind of jobs are we talking about?"

"Nothing that would require years of training or would jeopardize peoples' lives. Nothing like an air traffic controller or Neurosurgeon. But high profile jobs. Jobs that everyone always assumes they can do better than the people that do them."

"Like a weather man?"

"Exactly."

"What else?"

"Like I said, I'm just thinking out loud here. You've got to give us a couple of days to come up with the list. We can really amp it up. Publicize the hell out of it. Pack this place the night you pick the jobs."

"Speaking of this place..." John said. It was clear he was giving it some thought. "Who would run it, while I was off doing these jobs?"

"I would," I answered. "I need a job."

"I'll help him," Abbott offered.

"You'd drink all the profits," John responded.

"That's the price of chasing glory, my friend," Abbott said.

"And how do I win?"

"You win by not getting fired, and by doing your job better than the average person would do it. If you were a cab driver in New York City, you'd have to pull in more than the average driver on that route would. I'm not saying that would be one of the jobs. That's just an example. We'd have to evaluate on a case by case basis once you decide which ones you're going to do," I explained.

"What are the stakes?"

"What do you want them to be?"

"50 grand."

"50 grand? That's a little steep."

"I could be giving up over a year of my life."

"Your life isn't that great," Abbott deadpanned.

"Besides, you'd be getting paid to do it," I interjected. "Handsomely in some instances. Plus, you'd have income from the bar and probably a book deal by the time you were done."

"Not if I'm in jail."

"They don't arrest you for lying on your resume. They fire you."

"How about this? We start with 50 grand if it takes a year, but if it takes six months, it's only 25 grand. If it takes six weeks, then a percentage— like $5,700."

I thought it over. "Tell you what," I said. "Let's pack this place Thursday night. Make it an underground event because we don't want it to end up in the papers. We give 'em some food. 150 bucks a person. If we get 300 people, there's 45 grand, regardless of how long it takes."

The old man at the bar chimed in. "Put me down for a hundred-fifty."

"You already owe 400 on your tab," John responded.

"Then make my tab 550. I want in on this."

"And if I lose?"

"I didn't think that would be a possibility in your mind," I smiled.

"It's not really, but...every bet has to have stakes on both sides."

"How about if you lose, we throw an All-Day, Open Bar party here at *The Shanty* on you," Abbott suggested.

John nodded with no hesitation. "Ok." He shook both of our hands. "It's a deal."

II
~THE CHOICES~

The Shanty looked like the buttons of a too small shirt on a too large person—ready to burst at the seams. Music blared. There were at least three hundred people there. Could have been more. Abbott and I stood next to a marker board covered with a sheet in the middle of the bar. John was a few feet away taking it all in. The bar hadn't been that crowded since the night of the Hermosa Beach Open Volleyball Championship the previous summer.

"Good to see America loves to watch a fool make an ass of himself," Abbott mused.

"Far better to dary mighty things and win glorious triumphs, though sometimes checkered by failure; than to live in the ne-er grey twilight that knows not victory nor defeat," John quoted. "Winston Churchill."

"A fool and his money are soon parted," Abbott retorted. "Ben Franklin."

"It was actually Thomas Tusser who said that," I informed him.

"It is better to remain silent and be thought a fool, than to open one's mouth and remove all doubt. Abraham Lincoln," John winked.

"Whatever. Ok, Thomas Tusser. You're up," Abbott said as he motioned for someone to kill the music.

I cleared my throat and began. I wasn't used to speaking in front of crowds—especially not ones where both alcohol and glass were plentiful. "Thank you all for coming tonight to take part in our little scientific experiment. Is it talent that determines success? Or the advantages one has had along the way? Or is it a combination of the two?" I paused for a moment before continuing. "The rules of the bet are as follows; our friend, and owner of this fine establishment, John Mann, will be blending into five occupations over the course of the next year or so. A chameleon if you will. He can get the jobs any way he wants. He can lie. Cheat. Call in favors. Whatever. But if he fails to get even one of them, he LOSES the bet!"

The bar shook as everyone *roared*. John nodded sheepishly and smiled.

"If he gets the jobs, but gets fired, he LOSES!" I continued.

Another roar.

"If he gets the job, but they find out about the bet, he LOSES...And if he gets the job and manages to keep it, but doesn't perform better than the average person in that chosen profession would, he LOSES!"

A third roar.

"To be clear," I reiterated, "if he fails at even

ONE of the five jobs, he LOSES and we get an all-day, open bar, all you can eat, Roman Empire-style orgy filled with sex and rock and roll to be held right here at The Shanty!"

The loudest roar yet.

"But if he wins, he gets to keep every penny in this burlap sack totaling 48 thousand, one hundred and fifty dollars!"

There were some whistles and boos that time. Loud. But not quite as loud as before.

"Written on this board are ten occupations, which, at one time or another, I'm sure we've all thought we could do better than the people doing them. If we were only given the chance. Well, John Mann is about to get that chance. Mr. Abbott, the board please..."

Abbott ripped away the sheet and paused briefly for crowd reactions as he read each one.

"Number one! WEATHERMAN! Ah yes, the only job in the world where you get paid for being wrong all the time!"

He wasn't a meteorologist, but how much worse could he really do than they did every day?

"Number two! CHEF at a mid-level restaurant. Not fast food, but not fru-fru either. These are the places that have to survive by getting a niche or by having a hook."

To my knowledge, John's cooking background consisted of making a mean batch of Shoe-booty chili and boneless buffalo wings.

"Number three! ADVERTISING EXECUTIVE. At one of the big agencies in

New York."

Advertising was sales. Except you were selling to millions of people instead of just one. And if there was one thing John could do, it was sell.

"Number four! RADIO DJ. Any top 100 market will do."

A few guest DJ spots at the college radio station was the extent of his experience, but he was quick on his feet and personable.

"Number five! PROFESSIONAL ATHLETE! You pick the sport."

A college All American in the Ivy League was like being the world's tallest midget.

"Number six! TELEVISION SPORTS ANCHOR! ESPN, or any local affiliate."

This one had him written all over it. Sports background. Check. Quick on his feet. Check. Good looking. Check.

"Number 7! HIGH SCHOOL COACH! Any sport. Either gender. Any town. Anywhere."

This was another one I could have seen him succeed at. He had been a three-sport athlete in high school, and could have played any of a number of other sports if he only had the time. The question about this job would be how long it would take to succeed. He'd be looking at a minimum of three months, which would limit his time at the other jobs. But it would also probably be the easiest job for him to get.

"Number 8! HIGH SCHOOL ADMINIS-

TRATOR! One of the most unforgiving jobs on the planet. Can John be one of the few who is good AND popular?"

I could definitely see him doing this job as well, but it would require certifications and degrees he didn't have. He would either need to lie and hope he didn't get caught, or find a private school that was so desperate they didn't require them.

"Number 9! HOLLYWOOD TALENT AGENT! Has to be at one of the Big 5 agencies."

One of those jobs that pretty much anyone could do as well if not better than the people that currently do it, but a hard industry to break into. It would require knowing someone to break in.

"And finally, Number 10! PROFESSIONAL GAMBLER! By definition this job would be a gamble. Would require as much luck as skill. My friend, the floor is yours. Your choices please..."

John rose from his nearby seat and made his way toward the board. The room was silent for the first time that night.

He smiled. "They all sound so appealing, but...I'm going to go with *Radio DJ* for my first choice."

There was a noticeable buzz in the room. That one would be more difficult than it sounded, both in terms of getting the job and then being successful at it.

"You do realize that you actually have to be

interesting to be a DJ, don't you?"

"I'm interesting," John said defensively.

"Maybe to a couple of drunks and girls looking for free drinks."

"I resemble that remark," one of the drunks shouted.

"How am I going to be graded?"

"Simple. Ratings. Your quarterly ratings have to be higher than the person in the same time slot before you."

"Fair enough."

His agreeable nature made us both curious if there was something we were missing. Made us wonder if John had something up his sleeve. Abbott eyed him suspiciously.

"My second choice is...wait for it...A High School Administrator."

Everyone seemed to nod simultaneously. He had the personality for it. He had been forever accused of being a politician.

"But," John interjected, "I need the stipulation that it can be any administrative role. Superintendent, Principal, Vice Principal, Dean of Students or Athletic Director."

"Any objections?" Abbott asked the crowd.

No one seemed to have any.

"That one will be a bit more difficult to judge, however. I guess it really depends on which position you get. If you're a Superintendent, you need to come in under budget and save jobs. If you're a Principal, the standardized test scores need to be higher than the previous year."

"That will be difficult for me to do in a six month time frame."

"Then be an Athletic Director. That's easy to grade. The program has to run efficiently, come in under budget, and your teams need to have a better cumulative record than the previous year."

"Again, that would be difficult to accomplish in six months," John objected.

"Six months is all you have. If need be, we'll come down and observe, maybe talk to some people, see what you've accomplished and how you are viewed."

"That seems pretty subjective."

"Then choose a place where your impact is obvious. Or choose another occupation," Abbott offered.

"That's ok. I'll stay with it."

"3rd pick?"

"Professional athlete."

"Which sport?"

"Football."

"We are talking the NFL right? Not some pikey arena league."

"Correct."

"*This* I have to see."

"I was an All-American in college."

"Yeah. In the Ivy League."

"I had other DI offers."

"That doesn't mean you'd be good enough for the NFL.

"Maybe not."

"Not to mention you're 33. As they said in the movie 'Invincible', NFL teams need athletes, not 33 year old bartenders. And by successful, it has to be relative to the other players in the league, not Vince Papale."

"Got it."

Abbott shrugged. "It's your money. Next pick?"

"Hollywood Agent."

Abbott nodded. "Nice. I was hoping you'd pick that one. You have to broker ONE big movie deal. Minimum budget...$50 mill."

John mulled it over. "Just have to have a signed deal, right? Because it takes two years to make a movie. Minimum."

"Just a signed deal with a studio. With major stars attached. And remember. You have to work at one of the five big agencies. EAA, CAA, William Morris Endeavor, UTA or Paradigm. No little Podunk independent agencies."

"Ok," John shrugged.

"One more," Abbott said.

"Professional Gambler," John answered without hesitation.

The conviction with which he said it broke the place up. He didn't look remotely close to the part.

"You serious?"

"Absolutely."

"You know that in order to be successful, you actually have to *make* money?"

"I am aware of that fact."

"And that the casino is favored in every single game? And that poker is a game of chance?"

"Chance is what you make of it."

Abbott shook his head in disbelief. "One month. You need to gamble every day. Play whatever games you want. At the end of the month, you not only have to be ahead, but you have to have made enough money to live on."

Abbott then turned to the crowd. "Ok, folks. You heard him. Side betting is available if you'd like to bet on our boy, or against him. Or if you'd like to bet on how many of the jobs he'll succeed at, see Joe behind the bar. Daily updates will be available so stop on by. Any major developments will be sent out via email, so make sure we have yours before you leave tonight. In the meantime, drink up and enjoy the night!"

Money began exchanging hands like it was Derby Day at Churchill Downs. John seemed to be enjoying it all by himself, off to one side of the room.

"You know I'd pay a grand to see you pull this off. If I can help..." I offered.

"I appreciate that," he answered.

"Have you figured out what order you're going to try them?"

"I guess that'll all depend on what's available. But I'll let you know. And thanks."

"For what?"

"For the much needed kick in the pants," he

said with a smile.

III
~THE SEARCH~

Much like himself, John's one bedroom apartment above The Shanty was neat and clean, but largely unspectacular. His jacket hung on a hook by the door, and his keys were at the ready inside the lock, in case he ever needed to make a quick escape. The apartment lacked the soft touch of a female, instead settling for the bachelor staples of a flat screen plasma television with surround sound and matching leather couches. An autographed picture of Joe Montana hung proudly on the wall above his desk, and a trail of empty pizza boxes led to a refrigerator stocked only with bottled water, two six packs of beer and some leftover Chinese food.

Written on a sheet of paper on his desk in front of John was the tentative order he planned to attempt the occupations. He had "High School Administrator" listed first because of the obvious limitations of the school year. There was a negative and a positive of trying to find a position in education in the middle of the year. The negative was that there were very few open positions to be found. The positive was that whichever ones there were, were unlikely to be very selective.

After using several search engines, he found only three such positions in the entire country. The first was for a Middle School Principal in Dubuque, Iowa; the second for a Superintendent of Schools in Sioux Falls, South Dakota and the final position--the winner--was for an Athletic Director at a small, Catholic high school in Connecticut, located about an hour north of where he grew up. It also happened to be the same school where his youngest cousin went.

Located in the foothills of Bear Mountain in a picturesque area of Litchfield County was a sleepy little New England town whose main attractions were Sunday night Bingo at the Episcopal Church and Saturday night football at the local Catholic high school. St. Francis Prep, named for the patron saint of animals, ecology and all measures of despair, was the lone educational alternative to the 1,500 student public high school in town. Its' tuition was reasonable, but it was still a constant financial struggle for the families that sent their children there.

Like the people that occupied it, the building—the former town hall that had been donated to the diocese—was a bit worn, but had plenty of character. With only 448 students, having a diverse curriculum was a bit difficult, so

the school focused on the core subjects of Math,
English, Science, History, a couple of Art classes,
and of course, Religion. The teachers all came
from one of three backgrounds. They were
either lifelong residents of Salisbury who never
planned to leave; people just out of college
looking for experience before moving on to a
higher paying public school job; or retired
former public school teachers looking to
supplement their pensions with additional
income.

The athletic program was poorly funded, and
the teams, especially on the girls' side, were
horrendous. The notable exception was coach
Steve Pappas' football team. His two-way
players, with quarterbacks who also returned
punts and kicked field goals, had won five
conference titles and reached the Class M State
Championship game twice—winning it on their
the second try. For a while, the boy's basketball
team had some success, but the coach had
retired four years earlier to watch his sons play in
college. The baseball team had also shown some
promise, but its coach was mired in a very public
feud with the school's principal that left his
employment situation tenuous at best.

Keeping the ship afloat against a heavy
current for the past 32 years was Bob Sherman, a
fatherly figure, and that rare principal who paid
equal attention to academics, athletics and the
arts alike. But Bob had moved to Florida in an
effort to help his wife's ailing health. His

replacement had come from a private school in New Hampshire, a man who was far more comfortable in a classroom than in a boardroom or on an athletic field. He was not well-liked, by students, teachers or parents, in part because he was following an immensely popular man, but also because he lacked the people skills necessary to succeed in education. At heart, Dr. Kovac was a good person who really did have the best interests of both the school and students in mind. He just didn't have much of a clue as to how to express that. He needed someone to show him the way, and for a brief time, Pappas was that person. The school continued forward, in spite of the poor economy and all the other obstacles that stood before it.

But one mid-November night, all of that changed. Steve Pappas closed his eyes and never opened them again. He died in his sleep of a heart attack at 50 years old and there was a fear that St. Francis Prep would never be the same. The receiving line at his wake wrapped around the church four times and took nearly five hours to get inside. People had come from hundreds of miles away to pay their respects to the man who had almost single-handedly kept the school afloat, not merely with his success, but with his homespun logic and inspiration. He was a family man, and his family extended to every person who met him.

Standing in one corner of the church by himself, as was usually the case at any function that had anything to do with the school, was Dr. Kovac. He was saddened by the loss of his friend, and fearful for what would become of his school now that that same man was no longer around to help. It had long been believed that if they had not had a successful athletic program at St. Francis, the school would have shut its' doors years ago. As it were, enrollment had been slipping for the past several years, and losing the Athletic Director and football coach in one evening, would not help the cause.

Kovac had worked diligently to find a replacement, without much success. The position paid too little. The facilities were subpar. The talent pool of athletes was thin and many were thinking of transferring. Most of all, no one wanted to follow in the legendary coach's footsteps—not even his former assistant coaches. Anyone who seemed willing to take on the challenge was a person Kovac, the academic, couldn't relate to.

Ten football players transferred out within weeks, followed closely by siblings, friends and hangers on. The incoming class stood at 76 students and there was talk of the school going the way of the mill and closing its doors forever. Which is exactly when St. Francis turned his watchful eye to Salisbury.

IV
~THE FOOTHILLS OF ST. FRANCIS~

John flew into Laguardia Airport three days later, and made the hour and a half drive from New York City to Salisbury. It was the perfect time of year to visit. The sky, littered with a warm haze for much of the summer and early fall, had dissipated to clear blue skies, save for a few high, puffy cumulus clouds with temperatures unseasonably warm in the low-70's. The windows on the shops and diners in town were all open to let in the gentle breeze as people laid comfortably on the lawn in front of the gazebo on the Town Green.

John turned left onto Old Mill Lane—the single lane road that used to back up for miles on football nights—and glanced at the creek that ran below. The water was smooth as glass, save for a few geese that sporadically landed in it for a drink. His appointment with Dr. Kovac was at 11:00am. He was fifteen minutes early, so he decided to take a brief tour of the grounds on his own.

Walking up to the football field at St. Francis

now was like visiting a once proud city after the Empire had collapsed. The bleachers were rotting, and a few of them were missing altogether. The field had grass on it only in patches, and the uprights, looked as though a strong gust of wind could blow them over.

Inside the building, the walls were crumbling; the wooden floor boards creaked with every step anyone took, and the classrooms were ancient. The wooden desks were too small for the students to sit comfortably in them, and the chalkboards were so well used, that they didn't completely erase any longer. The dust in the rooms settled in the air as the late morning sun shined brightly through the high picture windows.

"Mr. Mann?"

John turned and instinctively held out his hand. Joseph Kovac was exactly how he had pictured him. Tall, thin and not particularly athletic looking, his pants were neatly creased, and his shoes were polished to a shine. He wore a navy v-neck sweater over a button down shirt and tie.

"Dr. Kovac. Nice to meet you."

"Likewise. So what can I do for you?"

"I was actually thinking more along the lines of what I could do for you," John answered as they began to walk down the corridor.

They toured the remainder of the facility before settling into the conference room in the main office. The gym more closely resembled a bowling alley than anything else. It was dimly lit, with wooden push-out bleachers, and a scoreboard from 1962. The court itself was long and narrow, and the glass backboards came down with the help of a crank and pulley. The bleachers sat behind them at each end of the court instead of on the sides as in most gymnasiums. The locker rooms were metal cages with wooden cubbyholes that didn't lock. There was little, if any, ventilation and that kept the air stale and equal to whatever the temperature was outside.

Dr. Kovac and John were soon joined by the two Vice Principals. Father James Connelly was a large, jolly looking man, a few years younger than his appearance, who had weathered years of highs and lows at St. Francis. He was a fixture there, in charge of academics and student activities. Ron O'Leary was an alum of St. Francis. A former football player back in the days before Coach Pappas, O'Leary had never been a great student nor one to bow to authority. It was ironic that he had never ventured far from something he wasn't very good at himself. He also had a rather sizeable chip on his shoulder stemming from the fact that he had been passed over for the Principal position after Bob Sherman had retired.

But the diocese wasn't about to fill the highest position in the school with someone who had been twice divorced and had a reputation for telling crude jokes in front of young female teachers.

"So, Mr. Mann," Kovac began, "What brings you to St. Francis?"

"I used to teach and coach a few years back," he answered. It was a slight exaggeration. He had helped coach a Pop Warner football team for a season, and ran an after school activities program at a middle school to make some extra money for two years. "Anyway, I decided I'd like to get back into it, and while I was researching it, I saw the article in the New York Times that talked about the difficult times here."

"Yes, we recently lost a very well liked colleague."

"And that the enrollment was down," John said.

"It isn't what we would like it to be."

"Is there any talk from the diocese about closing the school?"

Kovac was taken aback by John's bluntness. "We do have certain numbers we have to reach enrollment wise. They're giving us until the spring to do it."

"God created the world in seven days," John said. "Six actually, since he rested on the 7th. Father, you'd probably know that better than I. All I know is that you could build an empire in one year."

"While I appreciate your optimism, I'm not sure how familiar you are with the landscape and economics of this area," Kovac answered.

"I'm actually very familiar with it. I grew up an hour south of here in Milford. My mom's sister and her husband live in Torrington. And, my cousin goes here. Crystal Herlihy."

"Crystal is your *cousin*?"

"Youngest daughter of my mother's youngest sister."

"She's quite the basketball player."

"Taught her everything she knows," John replied with a wink.

"You mentioned in your letter that you thought you might be able to help us. I looked into your background a bit. An All-American at Yale? Does that mean you're interested coaching the football team?"

"Possibly," John answered slowly, knowing full well that he had no intention of still being there come next fall. "But thinking a bit outside the box, I actually have some ideas for the athletic program as a whole."

"So you're interested in the Athletic Director position," Kovac reasoned.

"Let's forget about positions for a minute. Turning around a program—any program--is a three-step process

First of all, the facilities. Let's be honest. They're egregious. Now, you can't make something old, new, so I wouldn't even try. I would do the opposite. Cherish the building's oldness. Wrigley Field. Fenway Park. The Palestra in Philadelphia."

It suddenly dawned on him that the three men in the room might never have seen any of those places. "The point being, people love character and tradition. Anyone can send their kid to a high school that crams 200 people into a stairwell between classes. Anyone can play in a gym that looks exactly like every other gym in the country. Make coming to the foothills of St. Francis an experience. But you do have to clean this place up a bit. Put some drainage and irrigation in the fields. Replace the rotted out bleachers and paint them. Improve the lighting in the gym and at least polish the floor. Clean out the cubbyholes in the locker rooms and replace them with lockers that actually lock. And for heaven's sake, fix the ventilation down there. It smells like feet."

O'Leary tossed his two cents into the conversation. "All of that takes money."

"I bet there are some alums who'd be willing to do some of the work for free. We could fundraise the rest."

"You mentioned that it was a three-step process. What are the other two steps?" Kovac asked.

"The second step is to get a quality coaching staff. Kids will travel to play for a good coach, as evidenced by your football coach. I looked at your coaching staff before I came down here. Most of them are teachers."

"Teachers are the only ones that can get out on time for practice."

"Besides, we like the fact that our coaches are also teachers. It shows where our priorities are," Father James added.

"Yeah. Losing," John said.

"Athletics are about helping make well-rounded students; not the other way around," Father James continued defiantly.

"Look. There won't be any students to "round" if you don't get this place turned around quickly. Like it or not, there are quite a few kids, both boys and girls, for whom athletics are extremely important. You wouldn't let just any schmoe teach A.P. Calculus. Why is it ok to let any schmoe coach soccer or basketball?"

The three men sat quietly in the room taking it all in. They didn't like what they were hearing, but they also weren't sure it was wrong either.

"What's the third step?" Kovac asked.

"Improving the facilities and bringing in good coaches will only get you so far. You need to actively go out and get the rest. I'm not saying give athletic scholarships and I know "recruiting" is against the rules. What I'm saying is, get out to the middle schools and sell

St. Francis. Sell its tradition. Its tight knit community. Its small class sizes. Its strong extracurricular programs. Then get them up here and have them go around with one of the athletes. Have them watch a game. Make them feel wanted. Do it on both the boys and girls side. You never know if some softball player, has a brother who's a star quarterback."

"We don't want this to be a jock factory," Father James said indignantly.

"Father. No one said athletes had to be poor

students.   I was a three-sport athlete in high school and an All-American football player in both high school and at Yale. Use athletics to build up the school, then use the money to build a new science lab if you like. The University of Notre Dame built its academic institution on the shoulders of the Four Horsemen."

"These ideas are great, but we can't even find an Athletic Director, or a football coach, much less a whole new staff," O'Leary said.

"You don't need a whole new staff. You need to keep the good coaches you already have, before someone else snaps them up, and you need to bring in a handful of other coaches that kids will want to play for."

"That's easier said than done. Unless, of course, you want to take on the job yourself?" Kovac responded.

John leaned back on the two rear legs of his chair like a student without a care in the world. There was a distinct pause of about twenty seconds or so, which was usually all the time he allotted to any decision, no matter how important. "That's why I'm here gentlemen," he said at last.

V
~THE MARINE~

Jim Hubbard was an ex-Marine who made his living selling therma-pane windows. With the occasionally stormy and unpredictable weather in Connecticut, it was a pretty good living. But his life, was baseball. He was an alum of St. Francis who graduated in the early eighties with none other than Ronnie O'Leary.

"I remember that goofy bastard when he had pieces of turkey hanging out of his mouth and couldn't tie his own shoes," Hubbard would say.

He returned to St. Francis in his late twenties, after his playing career had plateaued with the Triple A affiliate of the New York Mets. As a coach, he was a strict disciplinarian. If a player's jersey was untucked, he made them run sprints in the outfield for fifteen minutes. If they swore, they ran for thirty. If they were late to practice, they ran for an hour. And if they failed a test in any subject, they ran for the entire practice. The enablers of modern society hardly championed his methods. "No one wants to be personally accountable," was a favorite phrase of his.

But it was difficult to argue with his results.

His teams were successful on the field, and his players were respectful, disciplined and among the hardest working students in the school, off of it.

Without question, he was an acquired taste, whose brashness often rubbed people the wrong way. Early in the spring he had told Joe Kovac to "get the hell off my field", after Kovac had questioned one of his decisions in a particularly disappointing defeat.

"Get the hell off *his* field," Kovac grumbled to John when relating the story. "It's not his field. It's the school's field."

"He takes care of it like it's his," John responded.

"I don't care if he brushes it with a comb and sings *Moon River* to it at night. I want him out of here."

"Can I point something out without offending you?" John asked.

"Go ahead," Kovac answered in a less than inviting tone.

"There's kind of this unwritten rule in sports where you don't approach a coach after a tough loss, and if you do, you don't talk about the game. You certainly don't question one of his decisions."

"It was just an observation."

"Then reprimand him for what he said, and warn him not to do it again. Have you tried talking to him?"

"Would you step in front of a moving bus?"

Kovac asked.

"How about if I talk to him?"

"You can talk to him all you like. But the suspension holds while you do."

That afternoon, Hubbard stormed into John's wood trimmed cubicle that doubled as an office. "That little weasel suspended me! He didn't even have the balls to do it in person. Just left a letter in my mailbox. All because I told him to--"

"Get the hell off your field. Yes, I know. He told me."

"Well, it's true and it doesn't help that Helen Dempsey has it out for me."

"Our field hockey coach?"

"She and I used to date, and ever since I dumped her, she's tries to stick it to me whenever she can. She went and complained because I threw one of her little brat players off the outfield a couple of weeks ago."

"Why did you do that?"

"The ground was soft, and she and her friends were whacking a ball around with their field hockey sticks. They were tearing up the grass."

John rolled his eyes and shook his head. "You realize that if you're going to be like that, you make yourself a target."

"I know. I know. It just pisses me off when people don't respect property."

"All right. Let me see what I can do."

Helen Dempsey was in her early forties, a

woman who was pretty enough now to indicate she was probably *extremely* pretty twenty years ago.

"What can I do for you, John?" she asked as she sat down.

"I'm sure you've heard about the problems between Joe and Jim."

"Can't say I'm surprised."

"Here's the thing. I know Jim can be abrasive at times."

"At times?"

"Ok. Most of the time. But he's a good coach and he's a pretty good role model for his players."

"What does this have to do with me?" Helen asked.

"I know you don't like him, and I'm certainly not asking you to defend him. But try not to fan the flames. If not for him, then for the school."

She thought it over. "Ok," she grudgingly agreed at last.

"I appreciate it."

John knocked on Kovac's door just after 5:30. The school was essentially empty at that point. "Got a minute?"

Kovac looked up from his computer screen. "C'mon in."

One could always tell the importance of a conversation by the way John sat in a chair. Normally relaxed and leaning back, he was sitting straight up now, arms out to the side.

"So, I talked to Hubbard. And I talked to

Helen Dempsey. Here's my conclusion. I know he has his warts. And he certainly exercised poor judgment speaking to you the way he did. He also needs to learn to work better with others. I'd certainly reprimand him, and warn him not to do it again. But then I'd reinstate him. Because just maybe....you contributed a little to what he said by what you said to him first?"

John had learned in his short time there that Joe had only three responses when faced with a request. Most of the time his answer was, "Absolutely not." Very rarely he said, "That sounds like a good idea." Slightly more often than rarely he said nothing at all. It was his way of reluctantly agreeing with you without actually saying the words. This was one of those times.

"If this blows up, and he does something else stupid, it's going to come down on your shoulders," he said at last.

"Fair enough," John responded. It was his standard response when he knew he wasn't going to get any further than that.

Hubbard was waiting for John in his office when he returned. "I wanted to see if you had any news," he said, far more humbly than John was accustomed to hearing from him.

"I was about to call you."

"That doesn't sound good."

"It's not bad. You've been reinstated as coach."

"That's great."

"There are three conditions. One. Be courteous and work with people regarding use of the baseball field."

"Done."

"Two. Smile when Kovac says something stupid to you after a game."

"That will be a little harder."

"This isn't a negotiation. I've stuck my neck out for you."

"Ok. I'll try."

"And three. You're the new Assistant Girls Varsity Basketball coach. Congratulations."

"Are you out of your mind?! I've never coached girls."

"Neither have I. It'll be a good experience for the two of us learning how the other half thinks."

"Why can't we coach the boys team? I looked you up. I read that you were a helluva hoops player in high school. Milford High School's all-time leading scorer."

"I'm going to try and get Rob Murphy back to coach. But he won't coach the girls and we need coaches for both sports."

"The girls will be in tears by the second practice," Hubbard grinned. "You're out of your mind."

"So, I've been told," John said as he held open the door to the office. "I'm going home."

VI
~PUTTING THE BAND TOGETHER~

With the new school year just six weeks away, John needed to get his coaching staff finalized. Roger McCarthy had been Steve Pappas' right hand man in the football program for the better part of ten years. He had played for Steve at St. Francis, and returned as a coach after graduating from college.

He knew the system, the personnel, the traditions. He was a natural fit for the position. He just didn't want it.

"I appreciate the offer," he told John, "but like I told Kovac before, no thanks."

"I didn't know Steve," John responded, "but everyone I talk to that did, says two things. One. That he would never want to see this program go downhill after all his hard work. And two. That you would be the person he would want to replace him."

"I don't think so."

"I can only imagine how difficult it would be to take the sideline without him..." John said, his voice trailing off.

"That's not it. Well, that's only half of it."

"What's the other half?"

"Steve was a full time faculty member here. I can't afford to give up my job to come coach here for $10,000. As an assistant coach, I could do both. As a head coach, it wouldn't be possible."

John quickly mulled it over. "What if I got you more money?" he offered.

"Doing what?"

"Assistant Athletic Director and Head of Intramurals? Run a few after school programs and help me in the athletic department."

"Kovac would never go for it."

* * *

"Absolutely not," was Kovac's response.

"This is our highest profile sport and we need a coach," John pleaded. "A dozen kids have already left. Another ten are talking about it. If we get Roger, I think not only can we keep them, but we might have a shot at getting a few of the others back. The kids know him. They like him."

"We don't have the money."

"Sometimes you have to spend money to make money. If even three of the kids that left, came back, it would pay for his salary."

Kovac rapidly tapped his fingers on his right hand on his desk in thought. He ran his left hand over his face and appeared to be running some numbers through his head. Finally, he threw his hands in the air in silent surrender.

"Thank you," John said as he rushed from the room before Kovac could change his mind.

With he and Hubbard set to take over the girls basketball program, John set out to bring Rob Murphy back for the boys.

"We've never been formally introduced," John said as he extended his hand, during a visit to Rob's home. "I'm John Mann."

"I've heard a lot of good things about you, John."

"And I've heard a lot of good things about you, which is why I have to ask. Do you miss coaching?"

"Now and then."

"Why don't you come back?"

"And do what?"

"Take over the boys again."

"What about you? I figured you would."

"Hubbard and I are going to take over the girls. I think it'll make me a better coach. Or it will drive me insane. One of the two," he laughed.

"I don't know."

"Your sons are out of college. You could bring them in to help you. What else do you have to do besides sit around and get annoyed by your wife for the next thirty years?"

He seemed to hit the magic chord. If you could see inside Rob's head, you would see a man trying to picture the next thirty years with no escape from his every day life. "You make an excellent point."

The softball coach was a bus driver in town who had played in the '84 Olympics. She was in the process of turning the program around, having won a record twelve games in the spring. Boys soccer was also in good hands. The coach had been a fixture at the school, having started the program fifteen years ago. A native of Portugal, he spoke barely comprehensible English, but was loyal, hard working and well liked. The girls program, on the other hand, had won a combined four games in the past three years. The teacher who had been coaching had already agreed to stay on as an assistant if John was able to find a more qualified head coach.

Nelson Figueroa was in the St. Francis Prep Hall of Fame as a running back and field goal kicker on the football team. The ironic thing was that he had always been a better soccer player as a kid. But St. Francis didn't have a soccer program back then, and unlike his brother, who transferred to Housatonic Valley Regional High School, Nelson decided to stay and play football instead. He owned his own business during the day, but coached two travel soccer teams in town at night.

"What do you think about taking over the girls soccer program at St. Francis?" John asked him one summer afternoon at his warehouse.

"I think they're horrible," he answered. "I saw them play this year."

"They won't be for long. There are three basketball players coming in next fall that also play travel soccer. And I'm sure you have some other contacts in the community as well."

He was intrigued now. "I'd have to see if I could fit it into my work schedule. What time are the practices?"

"3:30pm."

"Would I still be able to coach the travel teams? I need the income. My wife and I are starting a family."

"You could do them at the school if you want, right after your high school practices."

Nelson nodded slowly. "Why not?" he said, shaking John's hand. It wasn't exactly the enthusiasm he had hoped for, but it would do.

Last up was finding a Junior Varsity Girls' Basketball coach. His choices, with the season less than a week away, were limited, and he settled on twenty-eight year old Melissa Baldwin, who had played two years of varsity basketball at Housatonic Valley back in the nineties. She had the added advantage of having just been hired by Kovac as an English teacher at St. Francis.

"I've never coached before," she said timidly, her thoughtful eyes a sparkling shade of crystal blue.

"Every coach has said that at one time or another. The only way to get experience is to do it."

"I hear basketball parents can be pretty

tough."

"You leave them to me. I'll make sure they're nothing but supportive," he assured her.

"New cheerleading coach?" Hubbard asked as he watched her leave John's office.

"JV Basketball," John answered.

"She know what she's doing?"

"Truthfully, I don't even know if she could identify a basketball in a lineup with a volleyball and a football, but she's sweet, the girls will like her, and she's willing to take the job."

"She's also easy on the eyes," Hubbard added.

"There is that benefit as well."

"What time's the parent meeting tonight?"

"7:30."

"Beer after?"

"I have a feeling I will need several beers after."

With Hubbard gone, and his office finally quiet, John was finally able to open the sports section of the newspaper. He almost wished he hadn't. Yale had just lost to Harvard. Notre Dame's football team was completing its' worst season in thirty years. The Jets had won two games. And the Mets had just finished the most epic collapse in major league baseball history. The soft knock on his door was a welcome interruption.

"Mr. Mann?" the young female voice asked.

"C'mon in," John said without looking up.

"I'm not sure if you know me. But I'm Shannon Brennan. I'm a senior on the cheerleading squad."

"Sure, Shannon," he said, folding the paper up and placing it on the desk. "What can I do for you?"

"Well, Mrs. Tonelli announced our captain today."

"And?"

"And she didn't let the team vote."

"That's her prerogative."

"She chose her daughter."

"She must have had her reasons."

"But her daughter wasn't even academically eligible last spring, and the only reason she is this year is because she flirts with all her teachers."

John had to stifle back a laugh. "I could be wrong, but from what I understand, her daughter has been involved in cheerleading and gymnastics since she was five. She's supposed to be pretty good."

"She's ok," was the quiet response. "But she won't make a good captain."

He covered his widening smile with his hand. Translation. She was good, but the girls didn't like her.

"Will you talk to Mrs. Tonelli about letting us vote for a second captain?"

"I could do that," John stated, "but I won't."

"Mr. Pappas would have," the girl protested.

"That's because Mr. Pappas was known to have a charm that could have melted forged steel. I, on the other hand, am not the possessor of such charm. But I can give you some advice, if you're willing to listen."

"What's that?"

"Life. Isn't. Fair," he said, pausing after each word for emphasis.

"That's your advice?" She wasn't impressed.

"No, that's a fact. My advice, is when that happens, you can make one of two choices. You can either prove the other person right. Or you can prove yourself right."

"I don't understand."

"How do you think a true captain would react to disappointing news? Would they quit? Or show up the next day and work twice as hard?"

She knew the answer, but didn't respond right away. "She would work twice as hard," she said quietly.

"Ok, then. It's your choice, Shannon."

"Ok, Mr. Mann. Thanks for listening, I guess."

*   *   *

John crossed through the cafeteria at 6:45 and found it was already more than half filled. When Joe Kovac called the meeting to order at 7:31, it was standing room only.

"We wanted to take a few moments tonight to introduce our new Athletic Director. I know there has been some concern as to the direction of the school in general and the athletic program specifically since Steve's passing, but we are extremely fortunate to have found a person to take over the program, who brings a wealth of knowledge as well as playing and coaching experience. In a short time, he has managed to get the department back up and running as smoothly as possible, considering the circumstances. This winter, he will even be coaching our girls' varsity basketball team. Ladies and gentlemen. Please welcome, John Mann."

"Thank you. Thank you very much," John began over the applause. "I wanted to take a moment tonight to introduce myself to those of you I haven't had the opportunity to meet yet, and at the same time, go over some of the expectations of our department. First and foremost, I believe playing a sport at St. Francis is a privilege. The expectations are high. We expect players to attend every practice and game with very few exceptions. Yours sons and daughters will end up missing family vacations. They'll miss parties. They'll arrive late to dances. And sometimes, they won't even make it to the dances at all. If that sounds like a raw deal, let me also tell you the benefits. Your children will have the opportunity to learn how to win with class and lose with dignity. They'll have the chance to work with what I believe to be the finest staff in the state. And they will have the chance to make some friendships that will last a lifetime."

"Not included in those benefits," John

continued, "is a promise of playing time. That is earned, for I believe athletics are a microcosm of life in general. And just like in the real world, where we don't always get the job we want, or the amount of money we want, or the praise we feel we deserve; it's the same way in sports. Your child may not make the team they try out for. They may not play as much as they want. And they may not receive the accolades they feel they deserve. It is during those times that I ask you to trust that our staff will look out for them not just athletically, but academically and socially as well. But please understand that while you have to look out for the interests of your child, we have to look out for the best interests of the athletic program as a whole, and unfortunately, the two are sometimes at odds with each other. As the year goes on, if I can help in any way, don't hesitate to ask. I do request, however, that you first speak with the coach, because they are the ones at practice every day, and they know the situation better than both you and I. If that doesn't work, you can come to me, but I have to warn you, if the conversation has to do with playing time, style of play or system of play, it will be among the briefest conversations on record. I want to thank you in advance for your support, and I look forward to seeing you on the fields and in the gym."

The buzz of parents stunned by John's brashness, more than drowned out the smattering of applause that followed. He didn't seem to notice or care.

"Mr. Mann," a young mother approached. "My daughter Kim Fullbright is on the girls soccer team."

"Sure. Nice to meet you," he said, not breaking stride.

"She kicks the best corner kicks of anyone on the team," she said, trailing after him, "but the coach doesn't let her take them."

"I'm very familiar with Katie, and while I'm no expert in soccer, don't you actually have to be in the game in order to take them?"

"Of course."

"Then her problem isn't corner kicks. It's being good enough to get on the field."

"That's what I wanted to talk to you about."

"Mrs. Fullbright. Did you just get here, or have you been here the entire time?"

"I've been here the entire time."

"Good. That way I won't have to repeat what I just said to the group as a whole. Have a nice night," he said with a nod as he continued past.

"Not afraid," Hubbard said to Roger as they watched from a few feet away.

"Not afraid at all," Roger agreed.

VII
~ROME WASN'T BUILT IN A DAY~

Crystal Herlihy was John's cousin by his Aunt Robin, even though she was young enough to be his niece or even his daughter. He was at the hospital the day she was born; the first person after her parents to hold her. He was there the day she took her first step. And he was there the day her father passed away after a prolonged battle with cancer.

John also was the one who taught her and her brothers to play basketball, focusing on the mechanics of the jump shot, instead of no look passes and behind the back dribbling. The two brothers had been All-County forwards on Rob Murphy's Sectional Championship team seven years ago, but it was Crystal who was the most talented of the three.

John hadn't seen her in more than five years when he walked onto the campus at St. Francis. He arrived in time for her Senior year and unlike past seasons, this year she finally had some help. A six foot one inch transfer center, who had been the goalie on the soccer team, now occupied the middle, while two freshman guards roamed the perimeter, but it was Crystal who remained the star. She was quietly confident, always respectful, and the hardest working on any team she played on.

Off the court, she was an average student, in part because her gifts did not appear to extend to the classroom, but even more so because her *interest* did not extend to the classroom. Socially, she leaned towards awkward, failing to understand the teenage fascination with the opposite sex. When her friends spoke of a "hot" boy, or even worse, how "hot" John was, she turned a crimson shade of red. She thought some boys were cute, but she didn't think about them that way yet. In fact, she had only kissed one boy her entire life, and he turned out to have such a scorching case of face-melting bad breath, that it soured her on future experiences. Where John was concerned, she supposed she could understand how girls found him attractive, but he had been like a second father to her, and comments from her friends about him made her uncomfortable.

The main vice in Salisbury was alcohol, for drugs had not yet found their way to the mountains of Connecticut. Crystal avoided the aforementioned, not for any moral reason, but because she had witnessed too many friends making impaired judgments while under the influence. Besides, John had convinced her that drinking would offset all of the hard work and fitness she did on the basketball court. So it was jump shots and Gatorade for her as they headed into the first game of the season.

"You ready for the big game?" John asked, when he found Crystal sitting in his office.

"I'm a little nervous to be honest," she answered.

"If you're not nervous, it means you don't care enough."

"I know, but I'm more nervous than usual."

"How come?"

"Because in the past, we were always expected to lose. But now we have a new coach, and new players, and people are expecting us to be good."

"I think people are expecting us to be better, but I don't know if they think we'll be good. We're still pretty young."

"Yeah, but the expectation is there. Even from the students in school. You ever have to deal with expectations?"

"Every day of my life," John lamented.

"How do you handle it?"

"I usually walk away from them," he said, putting his arm around her. "But you don't have that luxury," he laughed.

"So, suit up, cuz."

Once on the bus, John took a head count to make sure they had everyone. He found four girls standing around one single girl.

"What are you guys doing?" he asked.

"Beth forgot her sports bra, so we're taping up her boobs," one of them responded to laughter.

"Are you kidding me?!"

"We would never kid you, coach. By the way, do you have any more tape? Beth's got kind of a big rack."

"Oh my god," John shook his head and looked to the heavens for guidance.

"Girls," Hubbard grumbled.

They had only ten days to prepare for the first contest, which also happened to be against the toughest team they would face all season. Norwalk was the defending Class LL State Champions. They had height and athleticism, both of which were essential in girls' basketball where the game was largely played in the paint. They had been to four state finals in the last five years, and lost only once. Meanwhile, the only thing John knew about coaching females before he arrived at St. Francis was what he had learned from reading Pat Summit's biography. He eventually reached his own conclusions.

1). There were rarely tears in the men's game, unless it was from the coach crying at how poorly his team was playing. But women had to be handled differently. Some of them could take you screaming at them. Most of them could not.

2). If a woman liked playing for you, she'll give you everything she's got. Men couldn't care less. They played for themselves and the glory.

3). Women were more coachable. If you asked them to run through a wall, they'd try to. Men, on the other hand, thought they knew everything. Thought they didn't need to listen. So they usually didn't. 4). Women were not very creative on the court. If you told them to throw the ball from point A to point B, they would do it. But throw a full court trap at them or a zone defense they weren't prepared for, and they'd come to pieces.

John's problem was ten days didn't leave him with enough time to put in his own offensive sets and defense, much less prepare for anything the other team might throw at them. He focused instead on the basics of dribbling, passing and shooting and then was forced to sit back and watch helplessly as Norwalk ran his team out of the gym.

"When's the last time you lost by 32 points?" Hubbard asked shortly after the final horn sounded.

"I've *never* lost by 32 points," John answered curtly.

"And I don't plan on it ever happening again."

Hubbard nodded, impressed. "We going back? Or are we going to watch some of the boys' game first?"

"We're going to watch *all* of the boys game," John answered.

The girls protested.

"Why do we have to go to the game?" one of

them asked.

"It's so embarrassing," another one added.

Crystal sat in silence, knowing her cousin well enough to know his response before he even gave one.

"You have to go to the game because it's important."

"What's so important about it?"

"It's a rivalry game for them, but even more importantly than that, it's your chance to lose with dignity."

"There's not much dignity in losing by 30 points," the first girl said.

"Thirty-*two*," the second one corrected.

"Even worse."

"There's dignity if you don't walk away and hide," John answered. "The success of your season will be directly related to how you handle this loss. Anyone can strut around when they win. But it's how you handle it when you lose that's important. Besides, it's not your fault."

"Whose fault is it?"

"It's mine. I didn't prepare you well enough. But it won't happen again, I promise you that."

It was the first rule of coaching. When a team is overconfident, take all the credit and belittle them. When a team has lost its confidence, blame it on yourself.

John and Hubbard marched the team into the gym in full warm ups and straight down the middle of the bleachers on the home side of the court. They heard all the taunts.

"Sixty-two, Thirty!" *Clap Clap, Clap Clap Clap.*

"Airrrrrr-balll! Airrrrrr-balll!" to the girl who missed the rim on a free throw attempt.

Most of the comments, however, were directed at John.

"Nice game, coach!"

"You should have stuck to football!"

Taking all of this in, and laughing along with it, was the Norwalk Principal. John nodded as if it made sense. People followed their leader's example.

"Want me to start pummeling people?" Hubbard asked.

John shook his head. "There'll be another day," he said, staring straight ahead.

The girls, all of whom were now looking at their coach, learned the meaning of dignity that night as they followed him down the bleachers and around to the visitors side. It was a lesson meant to teach them how to lose, but ended up having the opposite effect. They wouldn't lose another game the rest of the season.

He had used the loss to analyze his team's strengths and weaknesses. They handled the ball well, had a little bit of size, and could shoot from the outside. The downside was that they were young, inexperienced, lacked depth, and didn't know how to win. And *that*, was the real difference between girls and guys. Girls needed confidence to win no matter how talented they were. Guys could win with no talent, simply because they believed they could. With them, you needed to guard against "over" confidence. Learning how to win would come with their first close victory, which they got three nights later. Inexperience would fade away with each game they played. Their lack of depth, however, meant they couldn't play an up tempo game for fear of wearing down the starters. It also meant they couldn't play high pressure man to man defense for fear of getting in foul trouble. He focused instead on the fundamentals. Press breaks. Running twenty-five to thirty seconds on each offensive possession. Making their free throws.

Every game they won had been decided by eleven points or less, and every team they played walked away from the game thinking they should have beaten them; but none of them did.

The JV team, however, was not having quite as much success.

"I am the worst coach ever!" Melissa lamented after a particularly humbling defeat.

John consoled her with, "Mel, you're a good coach."

"Good coach?! We're 0 and 16 and our closest game was 21 points!"

"There's an old coaching adage that goes, '*A dog has never won the Kentucky Derby*'."

"What's that supposed to mean?" she asked, puzzled.

"It means that the Kentucky Derby is for

Thoroughbreds, not dogs. And even the fastest dog, is still a dog, and it ain't fast enough to beat a horse. You've got a team full of dogs, Mel, and I'm not referring to the way they look. Hubbard and I took the best players and put them on the Varsity. I watched three of your girls trip over their own two feet during warm ups."

"But isn't it my job to help them get better?"

"Your job is to help one or two of them improve enough to help the Varsity team in a year or so. And you are helping them get better. It just takes time. As for the rest of them...well, as long as they are enjoying themselves, that's all that matters. And they are. My advice would be to set a few realistic goals for your team. Like losing by less than ten. Then pick out one game that you think you can win, and make that your state championship. My first year coaching high school basketball, we lost our first nineteen games. Our twentieth game was against a team that had only won three. They thought we were going to be the fourth, but we played that day as if our lives depended on it, and we beat 'em. That night, our staff celebrated as if they were bringing prohibition back in the morning. And I suspect our players did as well. The point being, once we achieved our goal, we forgot about everything else."

"And what happens if we lose that game?"

"Then at least the kids will know what it feels like to play in a big game. And every time they play in one after that will be a little easier.

You're a good coach, Mel," John repeated. "The players believe in you. And so do I," he said as he put his arm around her.

"Thanks," she smiled, as she rested her head on his shoulder.

"You coming back up for the Varsity game?" he asked.

"Yes," she said. "I've just got to put this stuff inside first."

After the door to the locker room closed behind her, Hubbard yelled over mockingly to him, "Do you believe in me too?"

"Yeah, yeah," John said as he dismissed him with a wave.

"Are you going to put your arm around me when I lose by ten runs this spring? Of course, that will never happen, but if it did..."

"Shut up, Hubbard."

When the Varsity game ended with another victory for the girls and a somewhat rare victory for the rebuilding boys team, the coaches of both programs met out for drinks after.

Thirsty's was the small town version of a sports bar. But instead of flat screen TV's and professional sports memorabilia, they had tube televisions that stuck out from the walls, which were decorated with jerseys and signed balls by the local high school teams. In a case above one of the tables, sat a signed football from Steve Pappas' 2007 State Championship team. That was the table they sat at.

"Eight and nine," Rob Murphy moaned. "Do you know that in all my years of coaching, at no point in any season, have I ever had a losing record before?"

"Well, you won tonight," John said. "And if Bobby Knight himself was coaching your crew, he would have a losing record too. But you'll be above .500 when it's over. I know it."

"We'll have to win our last two to do it."

"You will. Now what's everyone drinking?"

"A couple pitchers of Bud sounds good," Nelson Figueroa said. He had joined Murphy's staff upon his return to coaching.

"Drinks are on me tonight, ladies and gentlemen," John said.

"Oh, they're on you?" Hubbard asked with a smile. "In that case, make it a couple of pitchers of something good."

"There goes our Golden Boy," Rob said as John made his way to the bar.

"Why do you call him that?" Hubbard asked.

"That's what the parents call him. Driving his Mercedes, standing with his backwards baseball cap at practice without a care in the world."

"His Mercedes is 10 years old, and I'll tell you what. He's done everything he promised so far," Nelson said.

"That's true," Hubbard agreed. "He sure saved my ass. That a-hole Kovac would have run me out for no good reason if it wasn't for Mann."

"Well, you did tell him to get the hell off your field," Murphy said to laughter from everyone.

"One time! Geez."

"He had irrigation and drainage put in on the lower fields."

"He got new dugouts for baseball. And he replaced all the bleachers in the football stadium, along with new sod for the field."

"Not to mention had the locker rooms redone," Nelson added.

"To be fair, it wasn't like it was his money," Rob said.

"He's the one who raised it," Hubbard corrected. "Don't get me wrong, I loved Steve just as much as everyone, but he would never have butted heads with Joe so he could fundraise for athletics. Joe always hated competing with the annual fund."

"He even bought all new uniforms for JV girls basketball," Melissa added quietly.

"Of course he did," Rob said as the others all laughed.

"What's so funny?" she asked.

"AD's pet," Rob taunted.

"What are you talking about?"

"He *loves* you. If you asked him to wipe down the basketball court with his bare hands for you, he would do it."

"How old is he anyway?" she asked as if it was the first time she had given it any thought.

"Old enough to be yo pappy!" Nelson said to

laughter.

"Seriously."

"He's 33," Hubbard answered. "How old are you?"

"Twenty-five."

"Then to be yo pappy, he would have had to be one hellaciously active pre-teen!" Rob said as the table erupted.

"You're crazy," she laughed. "Besides, you should have seen him defending you tonight to one of the parents."

"He ripped Richie Magner a new asshole," Hubbard said.

"That's because he doesn't care. He knows he'll be out of here at the end of the year," Rob said.

"What makes you say that?" Nelson asked.

"C'mon. This is a vacation for him. He's not a long term guy. He's slumming in the small town so he can spend some time with his family. But he'll be gone next year."

"Well, he's here now," Hubbard said. "And I for one, am glad he is."

"Who's here?" John asked as he returned with the pitchers.

"You are. With our beer!" Hubbard said.

"Hey, John. Melissa was wondering if you could get her a straw," Roger said.

"A straw? For her beer?" John asked quizzically, before shrugging and heading off to get one.

The table erupted as she turned an embarrassed shade of red.

VIII
~A DAY IN THE LIFE~

"How are things?" John asked, peering into Melissa's classroom. He found her buried behind an endless stack of papers.

"No matter how hard I try, I can't seem to keep up on grading papers," she answered.

"That's because you're an English teacher. If you taught gym, you wouldn't have that problem."

"Too late for that now. And on top of the papers, my 7th period class is a nightmare. They don't listen. They don't do any work."

"Perfect. Less papers to grade."

"I wish I could be more like you," she said. "It's just so frustrating trying to reach them."

"You know what you need?" he asked.

"What's that?"

"A day in the life," he answered.

"A day in whose life?"

"A day in *my* life. It's guaranteed to make you feel a whole lot better about yours."

"Is that so?" she laughed.

"Tell you what. Tomorrow, I'm bringing you with me to the monthly AD meeting."

"But I've got classes to teach."

"I'll tell Joe we're discussing next year's JV basketball schedules and I need you there. I'll get him to cover your classes. Trust me. You'll be glad you did it once you see what I have to deal with."

The following morning, they drove over to the conference school that always hosted the meeting. It was interesting getting to see how the other half lived. Marble entranceway. Full computer labs. Student lounges. A library that actually *resembled* a library. They tiptoed past the reference books toward the conference room in the back.

"What time does the meeting start?" Melissa asked.

"8 o'clock."

"But it's 8:15."

"Yeah. I'm a little early today," he answered.

No one looked up when he pulled the door open to the room. Evidently, they were used to his late arrivals. A few of the male AD's looked up with curiosity at the sight of Melissa. The man in the front of the room continued to drone on.

"Who's that guy?" Melissa whispered.

"He's the AD from Litchfield. He's the Chairman of the conference," John answered.

"What's he talking about?"

"I have no idea. But he seems to have quite a captive audience. The AD from Torrington is sleeping with his head in his hand. The AD from Housatonic is drooling on himself. And I believe the AD's from Lewis Mills and Nonnewaug are involved in a rousing game of tic-tac-toe."

"Shhhhhh," the lady seated in front of them admonished.

"That's the AD from Terryville. She's a bit moody," John said just quietly enough that she might not have heard him. "Let's get out of here and get a danish and orange juice. They usually have it just outside the room."

"You want to walk out while he's speaking?" Melissa asked, horrified at the thought.

"Why not? We walked *in* while he was speaking."

"Yes, but..."

"It's ok. He seems to be talking about how to administer swim meets, and we have neither a swimming pool, nor a swim team."

Melissa followed him outside to where the breakfast spread was laid out. "Want some coffee?" he asked.

"No thanks. I don't drink it."

"Me neither. I like the smell a lot more than I like the taste. Kind of like deodorant."

"Can't say that I've ever tasted deodorant," she laughed.

"Yeah, you're not missing much. You ever see these interactive computer programs?" he asked while playing with a nearby computer. "They critique your paper while you write it."

"That would come in handy for grading," Melissa said.

A small, paperback book on a shelf caught John's eye. "I love this book," he said. "<u>All I Really Need to Know, I Learned in Kindergarten</u>. It's a simple, inspirational piece. You know. Share. Play well. Hold someone's hand while crossing the street. I collect things like it. Short stories. Quotes. It's kind of corny I know."

"No, it's not. I have a quote book myself. In fact, I write a different quote on the board in my classroom at the beginning of each day."

"Now, that's corny," John smirked.

"Hey!"

"I'm just teasing. What was yesterday's quote?"

"*Far better to dary mighty things, and win glorious triumphs, though sometimes checkered by failure; than to live in that ne'er grey twilight that knows not victory, nor defeat.*"

"Winston Churchill," he mused, and for the briefest of moments, he flashed back to another life. His *real* life, unlike the pretend one he now inhabited. But which was really real? The line had somehow blurred.

She broke the silence with a question that had been on her mind for quite some time. "How did you end up here?"

"I beg your pardon?"

"I mean, where did you come from?"

"Hermosa Beach, California."

"I know that. I mean, why here? You're a bright, talented guy. I could see you at a lot of places. CEO of a company. College basketball coach. Politician. Just not here."

"Why not here?" he asked, not sure if he should be offended or not.

"Because you're too talented for this place, John."

"Well, thanks. But everyone's got to start somewhere."

"When you're 25 maybe," she laughed.

He smiled. "Sometimes life gives you a do over. Besides, I'll let you in on a little secret. I'm not all that talented."

"You might want to get in there, John. They're talking about the division alignment," one of the female AD's said to him while pouring a cup of coffee.

"Ceil. This is Melissa Baldwin, our JV girls' basketball coach. Melissa, this is Ceil Donnelly, my favorite Athletic Director. Melissa is thinking about possibly becoming an administrator. Any words of wisdom for her?"

Ceil looked her straight in the eyes. "Run. Run as fast as you can. In the opposite direction."

"On that note..." John laughed.

"Do all the AD's like their jobs as much as she does?" Melissa asked as they returned inside.

"Nah. She's one of the more upbeat ones."

"Mr. Mann. Perfect timing," the chairman said. "We've just begun discussion on the

divisional alignment and playoff system. There
are three proposals on the table. The first is
taking the top four teams in each division into
the playoffs."

"Our conference is split into two divisions.
Large schools in one. Medium and small
schools in the other," John explained to Melissa.
"The medium and small schools will favor that
proposal because it would give them a better
chance of reaching the playoffs."

"The second proposal," the chairman
continued, "is to take the division champions,
plus the next six best records, regardless of
division."

"The large schools will favor that one,
because it would give them a better chance of
making the playoffs," John said.

"And the third proposal is to take the top two
teams in each division, plus the next four best
records."

"That's kind of the compromise plan."

"Which plan do you support? The first
one?"

"Personally, I'm in favor of the second one.
I wouldn't want to make the playoffs unless I felt
like I was one of the eight best teams. But Joe
supports the first proposal, so I have to. Joe's all
about division titles and making playoffs."

"Any thoughts, John, before we put it to a
vote?" the chairman asked.

"Well, I think if you went with the second
plan, there isn't any point of even having

divisions. You might as well just put the whole conference together and rank the teams one through eight. The third one is a decent compromise, but I think the first one is more along the lines of what the conference was founded on. Giving the small schools a chance to succeed."

"Which one do you think will win?" Melissa asked as they prepared to vote.

"The first one will win," John answered. "All the middle and small schools will back it. So will the top large schools, because they know they're going to make the playoffs, and when they do, they'd rather play the weaker, small schools. The only ones who won't back it are the middle of the pack large schools. It will pass 11-5."

Melissa counted the *yes's* for the first proposal. They totaled exactly eleven. "This must be what it's like on Capitol Hill," Melissa remarked. "Everyone's got their own agenda. Now I see how nothing gets done."

After several hours more of doing nothing, the meeting finally droned to its conclusion. "What are you doing tonight?" Melissa asked as they left.

"Oh, I have a busy night planned of watching *Friends* re-runs on TBS while eating a TV dinner. Why?"

"Would you like to come over to my parents house with me for dinner?"

"I don't know. That sounds as though it

might be a bit too healthy."

"C'mon. You'd be doing me a favor by not making me go there all by myself."

"I don't knowww," he hesitated before relenting. "I suppose one home cooked meal won't kill me."

The Baldwin's home was a colonial near the center of town, with a front porch that ran the full length of the house. Inside, the ceilings were low and the floors creaked with every step, the way all beautiful old homes did. A big vat of spaghetti, another one of sauce and a third one filled with salad sat on the kitchen table as John joined Melissa and her parents.

Mr. Baldwin held up a beer. "Would you like one?"

"Sure," John responded. "Sounds good."

"I've heard a lot about you, John," her father said.

"Good things I hope."

"Most of them."

"Well, a friend of mine used to say that if everybody likes you, you must not be doing something right."

"Very true." Mr. Baldwin was the original straight shooter. "So how the hell did you end up here?" he asked. It had exploded out of his mouth like he had been waiting to ask the question all day. "I mean, no one seems to know much about you. Where you came from. What you did before you came here..."

"Pretty simple really. I grew up in Connecticut, but I moved out west about ten years ago because I was tired of the winters. I used think about moving back because I've always been close to my parents but they both passed away a couple of years ago within six months of each other, so I decided to stay. But recently, I began to miss home. The only family I have still lives out here."

Mrs. Baldwin seemed to love the answer. Mr. Baldwin wasn't yet convinced. "But why St. Francis? There are bigger and better places."

"Dad!" Melissa said in protest to the line of questioning.

"My cousin goes here. She said the school began to struggle after Steve Pappas died, and I guess thought I could help."

"Melissa talked about going west after college. Thank god she met that jerk boyfriend of hers. Kept her on the East Coast at least."

"Dad!" she shrieked.

John choked as he took a sip of his beer, almost spitting it onto the table.

"John. Would you like to go for a walk?" she said, trying to keep her composure.

"Sure," he smiled.

All fathers were alike, John determined. They had no time for bullshit—especially where their daughters were concerned.

The temperature had dropped considerably since the sun had set, and yet, no matter how many times one had experienced it, the chill still managed to catch most people off guard. John draped his jacket over Melissa's shoulders when he saw her shivering.

"I'm really sorry about my father. He can be so obnoxious."

"You should have met mine," John said. "He loved me, but off the record, I think he would have told you I lacked motivation."

Melissa laughed heartily. "Why would you say that?"

"He just thought I had endless potential, but never amounted to much."

"What did he want you to be?"

"I dunno. Maybe Governor. I went to high school with Alan Huber. Little known fact. I was number one in the class. He was number two."

"Who's Alan Huber?"

"The new Governor?"

"Oh yeaaah. Maybe your father was right," she laughed.

"Thanks a lot."

"I'm only teasing. From what I know of you, John, you could do anything you want. You just have to figure out what that is."

"Enough about me. Tell me about this jerk boyfriend of yours," he said with a wink.

"Contrary to what my father thinks, he's not a jerk."

"Why does he think that?"

"Because the first time he picked me up at

the house, he didn't open my car door for me and my father was watching."

"That's it?"

"That's it."

"I'm glad I held the door open for you when we just left," John said.

"Believe me, I'm sure my father noticed."

"So how did you guys meet?"

"I met Jason in English class my freshman year of college. He sat down next to me on the first day and we talked a bit. But I didn't go again after that for about a month, because it was an eight o'clock class. Anyway, Jason signed me in every day without me even asking, just so I wouldn't be marked off for attendance."

"Big deal," John smirked, "I did that for half the football team at Yale, and I don't think any of them fell in love with me."

She smiled as she continued with her story. "So one day, we had a paper due, and I didn't even know about it because I had missed so many classes. Without telling me, Jason took his own name off his paper and put mine on it and then got an extension so he could write another one. I didn't find out until I went to see the professor about getting an extension myself, and he told me how much he enjoyed my paper. When I finally figured out what happened, I took Jason out to dinner to thank him and to try and figure out why he did that for someone he barely knew. And we've been together ever since."

"If he really cared about you, he wouldn't

have cheated you out of your education and told you about the paper to begin with."

"You do have an interesting way of looking at things," Melissa laughed. "And you certainly have the ability to make me laugh."

"That's because I'm funny."

They were both laughing as they approached the house. Mrs. Baldwin was on the porch. "Melissa. Jason's here."

Her mother sounded almost disappointed.

"Jason's here?! He came in from New Hampshire?" She looked to the driveway and saw the Prius with the "Live Free or Die" plates.

"Well, I should get going," John said.

The look on her face was one of frustration. She didn't want him to leave, but knew she couldn't ask him to stay.

"You know, John. You were right. Today was exactly what I needed," was what came out.

"I'm glad," he answered somewhat sadly.

She hugged him goodbye and handed him his coat back. He didn't bother to put it on, tossing it instead on the passenger seat of his car as he climbed in. Melissa stared down the empty road long after he had driven out of sight, before finally joining her mother inside.

IX
˜TO THE VICTOR GOES THE SPOILS˜

John quickly found that on an average day, he probably spent only 20 to 30 minutes doing work he actually enjoyed. The rest was a never-ending string of paperwork without the aide of a secretary or administrative assistant to help him with it.

"What can I do for you, Miss Baldwin?" he asked, peering up at her over the top of his computer.

"Just wanted to make sure you were coming to the big game today."

"I'll be there."

"I hope to God we win this one."

"Is everybody healthy?" John asked, before adding under his breath, "Not that it really matters."

"What's that supposed to mean?"

"Nothing really. It's just that all of your girls are equally bad, so it shouldn't really matter if anyone was hurt."

"Eww," she said, sounding like a scorned teenager. "I don't like you very much."

"Take a number," John laughed. "The line

forms to the left."

The game was exciting by JV girls' basketball standards, meaning a few points were scored and the referee only blew his whistle 126 times per half. The hockey team, and both the boys and girls varsity basketball teams even ended practice early so they could cheer the winless team on. With less than a minute remaining, a St. Francis player threw up a prayer that banked in off the backboard to give them a 32-31 lead. The last fifty-two seconds wasn't exactly Jim Craig versus the Russians, but a slapped rebound from the St. Francis center with ten seconds remaining preserved the victory and touched off an on court celebration with all the players and their coach—who soon thereafter ended up jumping exuberantly into the arms of the athletic director.

"Dinner and drinks are on you tonight!" she stated.

"But I had already mapped out an evening involving a TV dinner, a couple of Coronas, and my feet on the coffee table while I watch the Knicks lose."

"You can watch the game at *Thirsty's*," she answered.

John nodded. "I could do that. Let me see if Hubbard wants to join us," he said, reaching for his cell phone.

Melissa quickly put her hand over his to stop him. "Why don't you *not* see if he wants to join us," she said quietly.

"I could *not* do that," John answered, pleasantly surprised.

Off to the side a couple of boys basketball players watched with interest. "No wonder the JV girls' team got new uniforms this year," one of them cracked.

"If I thought she would jump into my arms like that, I would have given them warm ups too," the other one responded.

Thirsty's was even more crowded than usual for a Friday night. John and Melissa requested a back booth, far away from the parents that would inevitably show up to celebrate the lone victory of the season. The waitress wiped down the table and brought them drinks. She knew the orders for 75% of the customers without even having to ask. John opened up a napkin that covered approximately an eighth of his lap.

"I hate these damn little napkins!" he exclaimed. "So cheap. Spend an extra 15 cents. It's like those ultra thin toilet paper rolls that disintegrate when you wipe your—never mind."

He stopped when he noticed the somewhat horrified look on Melissa's face.

"So tell me, what made you want to be a coach?" she asked, in a quick change of subject.

"That's a tough one," John answered. "I guess you could say I kind of fell into it."

"How so?"

"I wanted to try something new and I had

always excelled at sports."

"Ok. Different question." She was full of excitement on this night. "When did you know you were a good coach?"

"I'm not sure that I am."

"You're 22-1!"

"A coach is only as good as their players."

"That's true. You did lose 19 games your first year coaching."

He grimaced. He might have fibbed a little on that.

"Another question."

"You are full of them tonight."

"Last one, I promise. Then you can ask me anything you want."

"Deal."

"Where do you see yourself in ten years?"

"I guess that would depend on who I see myself with," he answered. "We'd decide it together."

"That's a good answer," she smiled.

"My turn."

"Fire away."

"Same question to you."

"Well, I definitely see myself teaching. That's for certain. I've wanted to do it my whole life. I love it. Don't get me wrong. It has its' bad days. But I can't imagine not doing it."

"Do you see yourself doing it here? Or maybe in say... New Hampshire?"

He was obviously fishing around for answers.

"I guess that would depend on who I'm

with," she smiled.

"And how is Mr. Term Paper?"

"He's good," she laughed.

"Can you see yourself married to him?"

"I can," she answered truthfully. "But I can also see myself not married to him, and I'm not sure that's a good thing."

"You don't love him?"

"I love him. At least I think I do. But we've been together so long now, sometimes it's hard to tell whether we're together just because it's comfortable."

"I've always thought that's what marriage was. Finding someone you like as a person. Someone you're comfortable with. After all, the sex won't last forever."

"Well, I don't know about forever, but it can last a while," she said with a wink.

"That is more information that I needed to know," he said, shaking his head.

"I'm just kidding!" she laughed. "We're actually waiting."

"Don't tell me you're a virgin."

"No, I'm not a virgin. But, I made a decision a few years ago to see if I could hold out until my wedding day with the person I end up marrying."

"So you only have sex with people you *don't* plan on marrying?" John quipped. "Because, I don't really have any plans later on..."

"Shut up. That's not what I meant. And what about *you*?"

"Oh no, I'll pretty much have sex with

anyone."

"You know what I meant. How is it that you're still single? What are you, like fifty?"

He laughed. "I'm thirty-three, smart ass. And I'm going to assume your question is because you find it impossible to believe that a stunningly handsome, intelligent, athletic and charming person such as myself wouldn't have been snatched up by now."

"Yes, that's what I meant," she chuckled.

"I guess the answer to your question would be that I decided not to settle until I found the right person."

"And how will you know who that person is?"

"Some things you just know."

He walked her to her 1995 Saturn in the parking lot and opened the door for her once she had put the key in.

"Nice car," he laughed. "I especially like the rust."

"It gets me from point A to B," she answered. "Besides, at least I support the American economy instead of..." she nodded at his Mercedes a few spaces away.

"I'd buy American too if I could find a car that could travel 160 miles an hour, take a turn at 80 without spilling a drop of coffee or orange juice, with a 12 speaker Blaupunkt stereo blasting, while sitting in plush leather seats that are more comfortable than my couch," he answered. He lived in a shack and owned *The Shanty*, but drove a Mercedes. It was the Los Angeles way.

"It can really take a turn at 80 miles an hour?" she asked.

He loved that about her. She was as feminine as they came, yet knew about cars, and had no problem washing down a bucket of chicken wings with a beer.

John reached into his pocket and removed a handkerchief. He dabbed it on her right cheek. "A little leftover chicken wing sauce," he explained.

"You didn't blow your nose in that hanky, did you?" she asked.

"Only once or twice," he answered with a wink.

"Thanks for dinner," she smiled.

"You're welcome. You won a big game."

"Well, they were 2-16. I'm not sure that qualifies as a big game, but I'll take it."

"You did a great job with the team," he said, earnest now.

He extended his hand. "I never know quite how to say goodbye to you. With Hubbard, I shake hands."

She hugged him and kissed him gently on the cheek. "I'm not Hubbard," she said.

He stopped by his office on his way home to pick up a couple of game tapes. The hallways were eerily dark, save for the moonlight that came in through the drafty picture windows that adorned the passages. The only other light came from the direction of the library. As he walked towards it, the voices from within were clear and recognizable. He pulled open the door and found the entire faculty and staff seated in the back of the room.

"What's going on guys?" he asked.

The Head of the History Department came over to him. "We've been trying to reach you all night," he said.

"I was out to dinner."

Hubbard and the rest of the athletic department were seated together in the back of the room for this impromptu meeting. They seemed to be looking to him for guidance.

"What's this all about?" John asked again.

Maryanne Walsh was a bitter, recently divorced Math teacher at the school who was the faculty representative to the board of directors. With no family to speak of, St. Francis had become her life, and not in a healthy way. She handed him a two page document. At the top it read in bold italic print,

VOTE OF NO CONFIDENCE

It is the belief of every member of the faculty and staff of St. Francis High School that Dr. Joseph Kovac lacks the fundamental judgment, business sense and people skills to effectively manage a private, Catholic institution. His decisions to eliminate programs, raise tuition,

and his complete lack of tact and regard for the
students has resulted in a mass exodus that can
only be reversed by an immediate change in
leadership.

"Everyone has signed it," Maryanne asserted.

"Everyone?" John asked, looking back at the athletic department staff.

"Well, almost everyone."

"We wanted to see what you had to say first," Hubbard said, rising from his seat.

"Look," John began, "I know Joe's eliminated some programs many of you have spent your entire careers developing. And I know he can be coarse, abrupt, tactless and an all-around pain in the ass. It would certainly be much easier for him to always make the popular decisions. To always tell you what you want to hear. To always let you do what you want to do. But these are difficult times, and difficult decisions need to be made. I may be wrong on this, but I truly believe with all my heart that he has acted with what he thinks is in the best interest of saving this school. That isn't to say he's always right, but you won't know that unless you give him a chance. Now, I didn't know Bob Sherman, but from what all of you have told me about him, he was a great man, and if he were here, things would be different. But he's not here, so we have to make the best with what we have. I know many of you are upset at Joe, and that's understandable, but I think you'd be even more upset if the diocese closed the doors and you didn't have a job to return to next fall. Something like this might just push them over the edge."

"At this rate, we won't have a job anyway," one of the male faculty responded. "The enrollment numbers have been going down since Sherman left."

"And Steve," another member added. Everyone nodded in sad remembrance.

"I think we've managed to stabilize things," John said. "And in two weeks, we'll have next year's numbers. Give Joe until then to see where we stand."

"So you're not going to sign this?" Maryanne asked.

"No. I'm not going to sign it. And I would urge the rest of you to do the same."

As John headed for the exit, he heard a number of chairs shuffling across the floor. He looked back and saw Hubbard and the athletic department following him. It was an act not lost on him, especially given how much Hubbard hated the man.

X
˜HOOSIERS˜

The bus left at 9:00am for the 12:00pm game in Downtown Hartford. Forty-five minutes driving time, plus a forty-five minute break to have breakfast. The girls looked surprisingly awake for that time of day. They were also surprisingly quiet.

"Everyone have everything you need? Jerseys, shorts, warm ups, sneakers, socks.....*bras*?" John asked sarcastically.

The girls laughed, but it was obvious they were nervous. John decided he would save the big speech for when they arrived. The place formerly known as the Hartford Civic Center, now called the XL Center, was the 15,000 seat former home of the Hartford Whalers NHL team and current home of the University of Connecticut men's and women's basketball teams. It was also the site of all the high school state basketball finals for boys and girls.

John felt strangely confident about their chances. Not that he should have. St. Francis had never before been to a State Final in *any* girls' sport, much less won one.

In contrast, Our Lady of Lourdes was an all-girls, Catholic school from Fairfield County, rich in both tradition and success. They were strong in nearly every sport, but excelled in basketball. Dozens upon dozens of players had gone on to successful Division I college playing careers, and they were in the state final it seemed nearly every year. Their conference championship banners were too numerous to fit inside their gymnasium.

The two schools had met only one other time—at a Christmas Tournament in Waterbury three years earlier. Lourdes had won by 72 points, so thoroughly embarrassing their opponents, that several players from St. Francis could hardly bring themselves to school for three days afterward. When Bob Sherman had contacted the Principal at Lourdes over the lack of sportsmanship, the response was simple and equally tactless. "Don't put a team out that can't compete and then blame it on the other school." Lourdes had set a Connecticut State record for margin of victory that day that would probably never be eclipsed.

And although this was a different St. Francis team, with a different coach and different players; the question remained: How much difference could three years make? They had one common opponent. St. Francis had beaten Fairfield Ludlowe in the state quarterfinals by two points. Lourdes had beaten them during the regular season by *thirty*-two points.

John tried not to think too much about it, or

he would have been as nervous as his players. The US Hockey team beat the Russians two weeks after losing 10-3. Villanova beat Georgetown in men's basketball for the National Championship after coming in as 17 point underdogs. The New York Jets beat the Baltimore Colts in Super Bowl III. But none of those teams had lost to their opponents by 72 points the last time they played.

The yellow school bus eased to a stop in front of the players' entrance and the players laughed nervously as they looked down on the Class S final that was being played on the floor below. The arena was about half full, but he had a feeling it would be mostly full by the time they took the court, as it was every time Lourdes played. One of the girls pulled up for a 15 foot jumper, shot an air ball, and reminded John of his team's one true advantage.

He waited patiently in the hallway outside the locker room while the girls changed, tied pre-wrap in their hair, put on makeup, deodorant and whatever else they did.

It was a ritual he was used to by now, and he had learned to allot an extra fifteen minutes because of it. It didn't help that he was alone on this day, because Hubbard had scheduled a cruise with his fiancée long before he knew he would be coaching girls' basketball. It was hard to blame him, but it didn't help ease the knots in his stomach either, until the Ex-Marine who wasn't supposed to be there, suddenly walked around the corner with a broad smile.

"What are you doing here?!" John asked. "I thought you'd be in the Bahamas by now?"

"I was supposed to be," Hubbard nodded, "But I talked Jen into taking her mother instead. A Marine never leaves anyone behind," he said with a wide grin.

John couldn't remember a time when he was happier to see someone. Losing by 70 points only felt like 35 when you had someone to share it with.

"Coach. We're ready," Crystal said, sticking her head out from the locker room door. "Hey! Coach Hubbard! You're here!"

"Wouldn't be anywhere else," he grinned.

"We'll be right in," John told her.

"Any idea what you're going to say to them?" Hubbard asked.

"Well, I was going to go with *No one comes into our house and pushes us around*, but we're not in our house.Then I thought about, *I'm sick and tired of the Russians. Their time is over. This is our time!*, but we're not playing the Russians. Finally, I settled on, *Coach Hubbard couldn't be here today ladies because he's really sick. But the last thing he said to me before I left him was, 'Tell them to go out and win just one for the Hubber. I don't know where I'll be then, but I'll know about it, and I'll be happy.* Of course, you're here now, so that kind of ruins that plan."

"Sorry about that," Hubbard laughed.

"That's ok. I'll just have to go with Plan D."

"What's Plan D?"

"I have no idea," John said as he pulled open the door to the locker room.

Twelve girls fidgeted nervously on the benches in front of the dry erase board. Some made patterns in the carpet with their shoes. Others played with the zippers on their warm ups. Crystal bounced a basketball rapidly on the ground with both hands.

"Ladies," he began, "Some of you look pretty nervous, and that's understandable. After all, you are playing the number one team in the state. But I think most of you are forgetting the one distinct advantage we have, and I'm not talking about coaching; although I guess that would make two distinct advantages. Ladies, where do we play our games?"

"In the bowling alley, coach," one of the players answered.

"In the bowling alley," John repeated.

"But this place is nothing like the bowling alley."

"Maybe not at first glance. But where are the seats in the bowling alley?"

"Behind the baskets," another one said.

"Behind the baskets. And did anyone happen to notice on the way in if there were any seats here behind the baskets?"

"There are, coach," Crystal smiled, realizing what he was getting at.

"I guarantee you one thing. There isn't another high school in the state that has seats behind their baskets. It screws up your depth perception. Lourdes is going to be throwing up bricks all night, just like the two teams that are playing right now. In fact, there's going to be only one team out of the eight that are playing here today that's going to shoot well. You know which team that is?"

"The team that plays in the bowling alley, coach," Crystal said.

"Damn straight. And remember something else when you take the floor today. You're not just taking it for yourselves, or your parents, or your friends, or your coaches. You're taking it for the kids in the band, who may never get to experience a day like this. You're taking it for the girls who played at St. Francis for four years without winning a game. But most of all, you're taking it for Margaret, Beth and Crystal, who were on the team when Lourdes beat St. Francis by 72 points. Today's your chance to pay them back, and pay them back you will. The beauty of it is that you don't have to beat them by 72 points to do it. You just have to beat them by 1. Rudyard Kipling once wrote a poem called *If.* The last three lines of it are,

If you can fill the unforgiving minute
with 60 seconds worth of distance run,
Yours is the Earth and everything that's in it.

"Together on three, Ladies. One. Two. Three."

"TOGETHER!" they shouted in unison with their hands joined.

"How was that?" John asked Hubbard as the team filed out.

"Rockne would have been proud."

"Think it'll make a difference?"

"Oh, we're winning today," Hubbard answered.

John patted him on the back. "Thanks for coming."

The girls waited for their coaches at the top of the ramp. The lowest of the three decks was now filled on all sides. There were probably close to 10,000 people in the arena. Even John seemed a little surprised. And behind both baskets was a sea of gold and blue.

"Let's go, ladies," John said as they began the long jog down to the court.

"Good luck today, Coach," Rob Murphy said as he greeted him courtside.

"Thanks for organizing the crowd," John said.

"We made sure we left early enough to take over the baskets on both sides! Think it'll help?"

"It can't hurt."

Out of the corner of his eye, he spotted Melissa. Standing among the students, she could have easily passed for one of them. Jeans, navy St. Francis hoodie, sneakers. Even in the flurry of activity that surrounded him, he suddenly saw only her.

"Didn't think you'd be here," he said as he approached.

"Didn't think I was going to be," she laughed.

"I thought you had an interview in New Hampshire?"

"I did."

"I don't understand," John said.

"I decided I didn't want to move there after all."

"Why not?"

"Connecticut is my home."

"How'd Mr. Term Paper take it?" he asked as he gave her a hug.

Hubbard stuck his head into the conversation the way only he could. "When you're done playing grab ass, do you think maybe we could get ready for the state championship game?"

John rolled his eyes and suddenly felt dozens more upon them. "We could do that. I'll talk to you afterwards."

John knew the entire game and his credibility with the team rested on the game's first two shots. One for his team. And one for theirs. When Crystal's 18 footer rattled around and in and their All-American threw up an air ball from the foul line on theirs, he leaned back with a smile. St. Francis went on to shoot a torrid 72% from the field in the first quarter and led 19-6. The second was more of the same and the lead had ballooned to 21 at the half. Crystal had gone for 25 of their 41 points.

"Told you we were winning today," Hubbard said as they jogged towards the locker room.

"Game ain't over yet," John answered.

"You were right. They can't shoot here."

"They won't have to in the second half. It doesn't matter what's behind the basket when you're shooting layups. We're out of gas."

A quick glance at the team in the locker room was all it took to see he was right. Sweat was pouring off their foreheads. A few of them were still breathing heavily even though the half had been over for nearly five minutes.

"Ladies. Great first half, but it means nothing if you follow it with a lousy second. Now, here's the thing, and listen closely. You're not going to continue to shoot the way you did in the first half. Your legs are going to get tired. And they're going to try and make a run at us, but we're not going to let them. If they get back-to-back baskets, slow it up and get your composure back. If we need to, we'll take a timeout or two. When the third quarter ends, I want to still have a double digit lead. Anything more than that is great. Anything less is unacceptable. Crystal. They'll have two or three players running at you this half. Don't force it. If they're doing that to you, someone else will be open. If they're going to gamble, let's make 'em pay. There is only one more thing I have to say, and it's the most important thing you'll ever hear. When you get tired, do not allow yourself to get lazy. Move your feet on defense. Box out. Do not throw careless passes on offense. Teams lose games not because they get tired, but because they don't know how to handle it when they do. I've already told you what's going to happen this quarter. We'll discuss the 4th in eight minutes."

John was right on with nearly everything he said. His players did go cold. Lourdes did run two and three people at Crystal the entire quarter. And while they were able to chip away at the lead, John's girls never allowed them to make one of those game changing runs. The quarter ended with St. Francis still up by 11.

"Mission accomplished, ladies. We still have a double digit lead. Lourdes is not a good outside shooting team. They're going to continue to try and pound it inside. If they shoot sixty percent from the field, it would take them ten possessions to take the lead from us if we didn't score a point, and we will score. The question is this. Can you work hard enough defensively to make them burn fifteen seconds every possession? If you can, that will eat up two minutes and thirty seconds of the quarter. On offense, I want you to burn thirty seconds every possession before shooting. Take care of the ball. Swing it through with authority. Two handed passes. Step to every pass. That's five more minutes. Do those two things and we'll be sitting on a three point lead with thirty seconds left. At that point, it'll become a free throw shooting contest, ladies. Make 'em and we'll be state champs. Coach. Anything to add?"

"Ladies, I wasn't sure what to expect when I agreed to help out. I've never coached girls before. But you guys have more heart than just about any team I've ever coached. It has been an honor. Now, let's finish these bitches off," Hubbard growled.

With thirty-two seconds remaining in the game, St. Francis led by three. Hubbard looked at the clock. Then at John. Then back at the clock. Then back at John.

"What?" John asked.

"How the hell did you know?!" he said.

"I watch a lot of basketball," John answered as his best free throw shooter was fouled.

The one thing John hadn't counted on was Margaret missing both shots. Ten seconds later, Lourdes All-American had the ball on the wing.

"Jam the hole!" John shouted. But his players didn't rotate quickly enough and the girl banked it in. The lead was one.

Another foul with seventeen seconds left. Margaret again. The other coach called a timeout.

"Listen, when Margaret makes these, pick them up at half court. No fouls and no threes," Rick told them. The girls nodded. He pulled Crystal aside separate from the others. "If she misses one of them, you know who's going to get the ball, and you know she's going to go straight to the basket. Be waiting for her."

"Got it, coach."

There were two problems. The first was that Margaret missed both free throws. The second was that the All-American never went to the hole. She pulled up from behind the arc and drilled a three. It was the first time St. Francis had trailed all game. Twelve seconds remained.

Before John could even call a timeout the All-American stole the inbounds pass. Crystal had the sense to immediately foul her. The wheels were coming off.

"You shouldn't have fouled me, coach! Game. Over," the All-American taunted.

"Timeout," John yelled to the ref.

"I'm so sorry!" Margaret wailed. "I blew the game!" She was sobbing uncontrollably now.

"You didn't blow anything. Here's what we're going to do. Crystal, once she's on the line, walk up next to her and step on her toes with your heel. HARD. Make it look like an accident. Apologize and stumble a bit. Grab your ankle like you hurt yourself. She'll miss the first one short when she tries to extend on her toes. And she'll miss the second one long, because she'll try to overcompensate. When she does, get the ball to Crystal. They'll probably run two people at you by midcourt. If you get past them, you're one on one. Do you remember the first thing I ever told you about shooting?"

"Shoot the same way with someone on you as you would if you were by yourself in the driveway," she answered.

"Exactly. You're tall enough that they won't be able to block your shot without fouling you. Eyes on the rim. Hold your follow through."

"Got it, Cuz."

"Together!" they shouted.

Crystal did such a fine acting job after stepping on the girl's toes, that she almost had the other team and referee feeling sorry for her. And the All-American did miss the first one short. And the second one long.

"You know what?" John said calmly as Crystal raced up court. "You were right. We *are* winning this game."

Hubbard looked like he wanted to throw up. He couldn't even speak as she let the shot go.

"We're home," John said matter-of-factly a moment before the horn sounded and the ball rippled through the cords of the net.

Hubbard looked up at the scoreboard one last time to make certain before storming onto the court. It read, "St. Francis 58 Lourdes 57."

John never even left his chair as fans poured onto the court from every direction. He sat there by himself, with a smile that ran from ear to ear. But he wouldn't remain alone for long. The entire team—and it took most of them to lift him—hoisted him high into the air and carried him around the court. He laughed and waved at Melissa in the stands as the girls raced up the runway with him and out of sight.

*   *   *

"Coach," one of the reporters began in the

conference room, "How does it feel to be the Savior of St. Francis?"

"I'm hardly a Savior," John answered without hesitation. "I'm just going along for the ride. Here, some of the girls on the basketball team play soccer. Some of the soccer girls play softball. Some of the softball players have brothers on the baseball team. Some of the baseball players also play football. Some of the football players have brothers and sisters in the band. Some of the band members have friends in the drama club. Hell, the baseball coach helps coach the girls' basketball team. The point is, today wasn't about one team. It was about an entire community."

"Coach, is there any truth to the rumor that St. Francis will close at the end of the year?" another reporter asked.

"Well," John shuffled uncomfortably, "I guess that would depend on the enrollment numbers for next year's freshman class." He looked to the back of the room where Joe Kovac stood alone. Kovac scribbled a number down on a sheet of paper and held it up proudly. John squinted to read it in the lights. "Which if I'm reading this correctly, appears to be at 157?" Kovac nodded. "Then I guess the answer to your question would be a *No*. Looks like St. Francis will be around for a while."

"How about you, coach?" a fresh faced reporter asked.

The one thing John hated more than

anything, was to lie. Stretch the truth ok. Change the subject, even better. "I don't even know what I'm going to eat for dinner yet and you're asking about next year!"

It took several minutes for the rising din in the room to die down. Finally, a reporter's voice was heard above it.

"Coach Hubbard, you're only the third coach in state history to win state titles in two different sports. What is the main difference between coaching boys and girls?"

"Girls listen," Hubbard smirked to laughter.

Kovac waited for John and Hubbard to answer every question thrown their way, before approaching them. "You guys almost blew that one," was the first thing he said.

John reached out with his arm and held Hubbard back. "Yeah, we like to make it exciting," he answered with a smile as Hubbard rolled his eyes and walked away.

"Well, congratulations," Kovac said.

"Congratulations to you too. 157 kids. That's a huge class."

"Biggest one in 29 years."

"They'll probably make you a Bishop."

"I think you kind of have to be a priest for that to happen."

"Well, maybe they'll make an exception."

There was a long pause before Kovac spoke again. "Thank you," he said at last.

"For what?"

"For everything," he said, and John knew

exactly what he meant without him having to say any more.

"No problem. But I think I did fail in one area."

"What's that?"

"People still don't like you very much."

Kovac laughed uncharacteristically heartily. "Yeah, that kind of backfired. Instead of you getting people to like me, I think I made people *dislike* you."

"That's ok. I think we're growin on 'em."

John shook his hand and pulled him in for a man-hug. Kovac stumbled awkwardly, but smiled as he did. It was probably the first man-hug he had ever received.

Abbott and I had snuck into the room unnoticed in the stream of flash bulbs and reporters, each trying to out-shout the others. It wasn't until John finished speaking with Kovac that he spotted us.

"You guys made it," he said with a smile.

"Of course we did. Had to see it ourselves. And think what we would have missed. Congratulations!" I responded.

"So who's watching the bar while you guys are here?"

"Ralph."

"Ralph??!"

"Don't worry. We stopped by the fire station on our way out of town to make sure they'd swing by a couple of times today to keep an eye on things."

"I better have a bar to come home to."

"You will," I assured him. "But are you sure you want to? You seem pretty entrenched here."

"We have a bet. A bet I intend on winning," he answered. "So, since technically I am *both* a successful high school administrator *and* a successful high school coach, does that mean I did two jobs in one?"

"In your dreams, Mann," Abbott scowled. "This one counts as one or the other. But good job. One down. You've still got four to go."

"Where to next?" I asked.

"I have no idea. I sent out 20 query letters to radio stations throughout the country and received about 10 responses. Of those 10, two said they would listen to the demo reel I put together in the studio at St. Francis. One of them told me "thanks, but no thanks" after listening. I haven't heard from the other one yet."

"You've better find something soon," Abbott warned. "You've already been here four months. You have a max of six at any one job."

"I have a max of six months to succeed," John corrected. "It says nothing about staying longer if I already have."

"It says six months max at each job. If you can't get one of the other jobs during that time frame, you lose."

"My cousin is a program director at a radio station in Atlanta. I'll make a call," I offered.

"What are you doing?!" Abbott snapped. "Why are you helping him?"

"It's not about getting the job. It's what he does when he gets it that counts. And we said we'd help. Besides, maybe I've got a little side bet going?"

Abbott recognized that we all stood to make quite a bit more money if John succeeded than if he didn't by way of book deals, endorsements, speaking engagements, interviews, reality shows...etc. It was the American way.

"Ok. Ok. Make the call," he relented.

John's phone rang at that moment. It was a number he didn't recognize, from an area code he wasn't familiar with.

"Hello?" he answered.

"John. This is Scott McBride from KDAL Radio in Dallas. How are you doin?"

"I'm good, Scott. What can I do for you?"

"I want to apologize for not getting back sooner, but we received your demo a few weeks back and really liked it. The problem was, we didn't have any openings at the time. Well, now we do. Our midnight to 6:00am guy just left for a Chicago station, so I have two questions for you. One, are you still interested in a job? And two, could you get here by Monday?"

John glanced across the room at Hubbard, who was in his glory surrounded by reporters, and then at Kovac, who was actually smiling with a St. Francis parent. Finally, he thought of Melissa, who was probably waiting for him outside the locker room, before he gave the only answers he knew he had to give, "Yes...and yes," he said at last.

"I guess I'm headed to Dallas?" he told us in what sounded more like a question than a statement, as he snapped his phone shut.

XI
˜UNDER THE COVER OF NIGHT˜

Since he wasn't allowed to explain why he had to leave so suddenly, and he wasn't even sure if the reason would have been very well received if he had been, John opted to follow the path of the Baltimore Colts when they left for Indianapolis, by sneaking out of Salisbury in the middle of the night, leaving only a letter that said he had a family emergency he needed to attend to. And while he was fairly certain he had left St. Francis in much better shape than it had been when he arrived four months earlier, the thought did little to assuage the pangs of guilt he was feeling. But a bet was a bet, and he had quite a few people counting on his integrity to give his best effort—not to mention a desire within himself to see if he could pull it off, and maybe find himself in the process.

He had been to Dallas only once before—for a wedding—but all he really remembered of it was the trip to the hotel from the airport, probably because that was the only time he was sober all weekend. But he did remember that it had reminded him of two cities which he had always loved; Phoenix and Chicago. Phoenix for its warmth, cleanliness and sprawling suburbs, and Chicago for its' small town feel, wrapped in a big city. The fact that Dallas was a top 20 radio market told him he was fortunate to have been offered the job, but also told him that there would be high expectations. The fact that his predecessor had been offered a job in Chicago—a top five market--told him he would be hard pressed to improve on that success.

*   *   *

From the moment he laid eyes on Christine Fitzgibbons, he knew he stood for everything she abhorred in life. Humorless and motivated to a fault, her nickname was her actual name, once you switched the first letter of her last name with one a bit earlier in the alphabet. She was as pretty as she allowed herself to be; which is to say that should could have been pretty if she did *anything* with her hair, wore even the slightest bit of makeup and dressed in clothes that didn't look like they were pulled from the grab bag bin at Goodwill.

"So, what's the plan?" were the first words she spoke to him.

"The plan?" John asked.

"For the show? What songs are you going to play? What topics are you going to talk about? I've always found it best to map it out one hour at a time."

"I was just going to play a few tunes, then take

some calls and see where that led me."

"You're joking, right? People are always telling me I don't have a sense of humor. But you're obviously joking, and I get that, so that must mean I have a sense of humor after all. You *are* joking, right?"

"I don't think so?"

Her skin turned from an off-white to a shade of deep crimson in an instant. "Look, I don't know what it was like in Sheboygan or wherever it is you came from, but in Dallas, we don't *wing it.* We prepare or people get fired."

When John continued to stare blankly at her, she stormed off. "I can't work like this!"

Even the closed door of Scott McBride's office could not keep in the sounds of her ranting. "Where'd you find this guy, Scott? Because he sure as hell is not a professional."

"I listened to his reel. He's good," Scott responded calmly.

"He wants to wing it in his first show."

"Then let him. Who cares? It's the midnight shift. No one will be listening anyway. If he stinks, we'll let him go, and then you can sift through the pile of 100 demos I have stacked in the corner and pick out the person you want to work with."

It was kind of a backhanded defense that John didn't find particularly encouraging.

"Did I say something wrong?" he asked the man who was witness to the entire conversation.

Brian Humpal was the nighttime Sound

Technician at the station. Goateed, with tight curly hair and glasses, he possessed an understated, but much appreciated sense of humor. "Nah. She must really like you. She punched the last guy before you right in the face on his first day. Knocked him down flat in the bullpen over there," he answered, pointing to the other side of the room.

*   *   *

The red light in the studio went on at exactly midnight and John paused just long enough to make everyone nervous, before he began to speak. "It's a shade after midnight and you've got The Greatest Mann in the World coming at you on 104.1 K-D-A-L. The phone lines are open. Give me a ring. But before we take any calls, here's a song none of you will think you know, but all of you do know, by David Gray. It's Babylon on K-Dal."

"The first call is a relationship question," the voice in his earpiece said.

"You're on the air," John said once the song had ended.

"Hi John. I need some advice. I'm supposed to be getting married in a couple of weeks, but the other day, I walked in on my brother and my fiancée having sex in our kitchen. What should I do?"

"Let me ask you something. What did you do when you walked in on them?"

"Nothing. I was in shock."

"And after that, did you confront them?"

"No."

"Did they see you walk in?"

"I'm not sure. I don't think so."

John thought it over briefly. "Ok, that'll work. Is your brother married?"

"Yeah."

"And is your fiancée on the pill?"

"Yeah."

"Perfect."

"Don't say a word to either of them. Just switch her birth control pills with sugar pills and watch the fireworks display."

"That's it?"

"It will be plenty, trust me."

"So I shouldn't stay with her?"

"Uh...no. In fact, I wish all my problems were as easy to solve as yours. Run for the hills, my man, and give thanks to God every single night that you found out before you married that little whoo-er and she got half."

John pushed a sound effect button that made the noise of someone getting hit over the head with a frying pan.

The next call was about the Cowboys.

"Hey, John. What do you think the Cowboys need to do to make a serious run at the Super Bowl?"

"First of all, they need to make sure their quarterback completes more passes on the field than off of it. Hopefully, being married to Miss

Arkansas will help. I mean, who did he think he was? Did he really need to bang half of Hollywood? And what did these women see in him? There are at least seven other quarterbacks in the league who have won a Super Bowl. Why didn't they bang them first? I mean, at least Hollywood has a hierarchy. You don't get to bang Angelina Jolie unless you're Brad Pitt. Johnny Clipper only got to hit Joely Beckett while his career was hot. Once it faded, poof, she was gone. But the NFL is different. Even for coaches. It's the only league in the world where you can get fired for doing a crappy job and get rewarded with a better one. Pete Newell was a bum in Buffalo, and got hired by Dallas. Mark Mancuso got fired by the Jets and the Jags hired him less than a week later. And he went 4-12. Did they really think he was going to stop sucking? I've got a news flash for all NFL owners. Some guys have an *infinite* amount of sucking in them."

The guys in the control booth were rolling at that point. "Political call next," the voice in his earpiece said, barely able to get it out over the laughter.

"What do you think the biggest problem our country is faced with right now?" the caller asked.

"You mean besides constant terrorist threats, 12% unemployment and an ever burgeoning national debt?"

"Yeah, who's responsible? Everyone blames everyone else."

"The answer is...the system is responsible. We've got a good old boys network making backroom, sweetheart deals that pad their wallets for votes, at the expense of the people they work for."

"So you think term limits is the answer?"

"I'm not opposed to term limits in theory," John said, "If two terms is good enough for the President, then it should be more than enough for Congress. But everyone thinks that's the answer, and it isn't. If I knew my time in Congress was limited, I'd make as much money as I could during the time I had. And here's the thing. We already have term limits. We just don't enforce them. It's called *an election.* You want them out? Vote them out. I have a feeling if voter turnout was 98% instead of 51%, Congress would look quite a bit different. The answer is making it easier for people to vote. But the real reason I'm not opposed to term limits, is because someday soon, one of these old boys is going to drop dead right there on the Senate Floor, and I don't think that would inspire a lot of confidence from the American public."

"Next caller wants some advice on buying a car," the voice from within told him.

"You're on the air with The Greatest Mann in the World."

"Yeah, I'm thinking of buying a new car."

"What are you looking at getting?" John asked.

"A Honda Civic. What do you know about them?"

"I know they're a good car. Reliable. They'll run forever and they're good on gas mileage."

"I was thinking about getting one and putting a dual chrome exhaust system on it with new rims, tinted windows, a spoiler on the back and louvers on the hood."

"Maybe hang a pair of fuzzy dice from the rear view mirror? Paint some flames on the sides?"

"Exactly."

"C'mon," John admonished. "Don't be that guy."

"What guy?"

"The guy who buys a $20,000 car and puts $30,000 worth of accessories on it. Why don't you just buy a $50,000 Mercedes and actually have a shot at getting laid once in a while?"

*   *   *

"Great show!" Humpal shouted at him down the hall after it was over..

"Thanks, buddy. It was fun," John responded.

"Say, a bunch of us are going out tomorrow night downtown. Why don't you join us?"

"I dunno. I'm just getting settled in. I've got some unpacking to do."

"C'mon. It'll be fun. You can unpack anytime."

"Tell you what. I'll go if Christine goes."

"There's a greater chance of the moon falling

from the sky," Humpal said.

"How bout it, Fitzgibbo?" John asked playfully.

"How about what?" she answered sternly.

"How about going out tomorrow night with the group? They don't think you'll do it. But I told them you had a helluva sense of humor and would."

"Can I talk to you a minute?" she asked, pulling him aside.

"Sure."

Once she had him out of earshot she said, "How dare you try to make me look like a bitch in front of the entire crew."

"I don't have to *try* and do anything. You do just fine in that area all by yourself."

She reached out and slapped a stunned John across the face and walked away.

"Like I said, she must really like you," Humpal said.

"Yes, I know. She punched the last guy," John said, rubbing his cheek.

* * *

Humpal buried his head in the cleavage of the shot girl and pulled the glass out with his mouth. He then threw his head back and downed it in an instant to the cheers of the crowd.

"What are you looking at?" he asked John when he saw him glancing out the nearby window.

"I was just checking to see if the moon was

still in the sky," he answered as he motioned to the other end of the bar where Christine was standing. Her hair was still pulled tightly in a bun on top of her head, but she had on jeans and a form-fitting sweater with a little make-up to boot. "I'm not even going to ask what brought about the change of heart. I'm just glad you're here."

"What are you drinking?" Humpal asked her.

"What were you just drinking?" she answered.

John didn't hesitate. He motioned to the bartender for a shot of Tequila and nestled it between Humpal's jeans and his boxers. Christine glanced at him in passing, then dropped to her knees and pulled the glass out.

The place went wild. In five years, she had never so much as shown up at a Christmas party, much less done something like that.

"Somebody give her a chaser!" Humpal said as one of the others handed him a glass, which he passed on to her.

She took a generous swig before clutching her throat and gasping. "What the hell was that?!"

"Vodka," the person said sheepishly, trying to stay just out of reach of her right cross.

"I thought it was water!" she said before breaking into laughter.

"Who chases Tequila with Vodka, you jackass?!" Humpal said, smacking the kid on the back of his head.

"It was all I had."

It worked. An hour later, John convinced her to let her hair down—literally—and she obliged.

"I think you got a shot with her," he told Humpal. "She didn't even hesitate pulling that shot out of your pants. If it was me, she would have tried to bite it off."

"She does look pretty good," Humpal admitted.

"She'll look even better in a few more drinks," John said, raising a glass with him.

The chant began slowly and quietly at first, then gradually increased in speed and volume. "Buuttt-crack! Buuttt—crack! Buuttt-crack! Buuttt-crack!"

"What are they saying?" Christine asked.

"I have no idea," John answered.

The chant continued to grow, and Humpal allowed it to increase to a dull roar before raising his hand to quiet the crowd. He vaulted himself atop the bar and began swaying back and forth to the chant that had started once again. He unbuckled his belt and tossed it behind him. He untucked his shirt and tied it into a knot in front. Slowly, a few millimeters at a time, he began to lower his pants until his butt-crack magically appeared. He was swinging in full motion now to the delight of the hysterical crowd. Even Christine seemed to be enjoying it. So much so that she joined him on the bar in the same rhythmic swaying motion, while the top of her

butt-crack—covered gently by a red thong—
became visable.   Even Humpal knew he had
been beaten.

"My world no longer makes sense to me,"
John said to no one in particular as he shook his
head.

XII
~THE REAL KING OF LATE NIGHT~

They had arrived together, but did their best to make it look like they hadn't. Christine entered first, looking a bit disheveled. Her hair was back in a bun, but instead of it being a tight one directly on top of her head, it more or less flopped from side to side as she walked. She wore glasses instead of her usual contacts and a buttoned-down Polo that was a few sizes too large, although she tried to conceal that by rolling up the sleeves and tucking it in. She walked silently past the masses in the bullpen and directly to her office, where she closed the door behind her.

Humpal entered a few minutes later with a spring in his step and a mischievous grin on his face. He didn't say anything either as he sat down at his cubicle, although he felt 10 sets of eyes on him.

"Well???" John asked.

"A gentleman doesn't kiss and tell," Humpal responded. "But if you insist," he continued with only a moment's hesitation and no further prodding as the others pulled their chairs in a tight semi-circle around him. "So we go back to her place, nice place I might add, although it looks a bit like a museum. I don't think anyone had been in at least five of the rooms in three or four years. Until last night, of course..."

"Get out! You hit it?"

"In pretty much every room of the house. We were watching some B movie on TV and I thought I was pretty smooth when I put my arm around her. So we start fooling around, but I wasn't sure what to expect. I get her sweater off, and damn if her body wasn't ridiculously nice. Keep in mind she hasn't said a word in about five minutes, before she turns to me and says, 'How do you want it? Tell me how you like it, Brian, cuz I'll do it any way you like. Getting taken from behind is my favorite.'"

John nearly exploded from his chair. "She's a dirty talker?"

"Nooooo!" the others all said in unison.

"Like a porn star. So naturally, this catches me a bit off guard so I start laughing."

"You laughed? And lived to tell about it?"

"Well, kind of under my breath—" he narrated before being interrupted.

Christine stood in the doorway of her office. "I have to be on a conference call in a couple of minutes. I'd be forever grateful if someone would get me a cup of coffee," she said.

"How do you *want* it?" one of the female production assistants asked in her sexiest voice, as the others attempted rather unsuccessfully to stifle back laughter.

"Black. And thanks," Christine answered, eyeing them all curiously, before going back inside.

John took the cup of coffee from the girl and brought it to her himself.

"Thanks," she said, barely looking up.

"I'm glad you came out last night."

"Why? So you guys could have endless fodder for the next several weeks?"

"What are you talking about?"

"Do you think I'm stupid?"

"No, I don't. But for what it's worth, Humpal said it was the best sex he ever had."

"I don't care what Humpal—really?"

"Really. But the best thing about last night is for a few hours, you removed that gigantic chip that usually resides on your shoulder and let people in."

"And why do you think that chip is there?"

"Because you feel like you've been shortchanged in life?"

She nods, but doesn't say a word.

"And maybe you have been, but I'll tell you the reason why."

"Please do," she said wryly.

"You're talented. Everyone knows that. But that's not enough. Success is 1/3 talent, 1/3 who you know, and 1/3 how you get along with who you know. I bet Scott keeps you on the midnight show at a pretty good rate, because he doesn't want you to go somewhere else. But at the same time, he doesn't promote you to the drive-time shows because he knows no one wants to work with you."

"And what makes you such an expert on people?"

"You don't bartend as many years as I have without getting to know people."

"You were a freaking bartender?!" she exclaimed.

"What did you think I did before I came here?"

"I don't know. Maybe something in radio?"

"Nah. I was actually a high school athletic director and girls basketball coach."

"Oh my god."

"Anyway, I think you have limitless potential. And for what it's worth, I think if you would only meet people halfway, you'd probably end up producing the Evening News someday for one of the networks."

She softened a little. "Thank you."

"Of course you'd probably get there a little quicker if you showed people your red lace thong a bit more often," he added, narrowly sidestepping the pen she had hurled at him.

*   *   *

"What do you think of the BCS in college football?" a caller asked.

"I think it's awful. Even the old way was better. At least then three or four games all meant something. Now, only one game does, even though it's not necessarily the best two teams playing in it. They talk about incredible television ratings for the 'so-called' National Championship game, but they don't talk about how crappy the ratings are for the other 35 bowl games. The answer is to have a playoff. 16 teams, not this 4 team playoff they're talking about, so no one can argue. If there's any grey area about you being selected in the top 16, you don't deserve to be there. Then use the bowls. 15 of them. Eight for the first round. Four for the quarters. Two for the semis. And one for the National Championship game. Rotate who gets what. Have the semifinals on New Year's Day. And if you want to still have the other 20 bowls for the crap teams, knock yourself out. People will argue that it is too many games, but some teams play 14 now as it is. So cut the regular season back to ten games and most teams will end up playing even fewer games. Not to mention that the bowl games would all fall when the colleges are on winter break, so they wouldn't be missing any class."

*   *   *

"The other day, you said you think the system is what's wrong with this country. But how do we fix things? How do we get out of debt?"

"The answer is a flat tax. 11%. 15%. Whatever they think is fair. And then don't give anyone any write-offs. That way, the government knows approximately how much money they will be able to raise. It will help with the budget and deficit. Should someone making 20 million dollars pay more taxes than someone making 25 grand? Absolutely. And they would. They just shouldn't be paying a higher *percentage* of it. Some people will argue that charities will suffer if there are no write-offs. But I would argue that people will donate if they have some extra money in their pockets at the end of the year, which they would this way. If they find that charities are suffering, the government can allocate some money towards them."

       *   *   *

"I haven't had a date in ages. Where do I go to meet people?" a caller asked.

"Well, some people would argue that bars are the worst place, but I think it depends on the kind of bar. Smaller, comfortable ones where music isn't blaring can be good places. You could also try online at those dating sites. I know a lot of people who have had some success with them. They enable you to sort through hundreds of women until you find the right match, without having to go through the obligatory BS of a first date where you inevitably find out the two of you have nothing in common."

"What if their pictures aren't current or even of them?"

"That's certainly a possibility. That's why you send in a runner to find out what she looks like before you enter the place you're meeting her. The answer, however, is to go after thirty-something women. It's like fishing in a barrel with a shotgun. They're either desperate to get married because they never have been, or they're divorced with baggage, in which case they're desperate as well. You can try for the twenty-five year olds, but you better have a fat wallet if you're going to go that route."

*   *   *

And so it went. John's "schtick" was that he could talk to anyone about anything. It was perhaps his greatest gift in life. Need someone to schmooze a room full of doctors? He was your man. Someone to talk football to a crew of construction workers? No problem. Politics with stuffy college professors? Piece of cake. He was self-described as someone who "knew a little bit about everything, although not a lot about anything."

Because of that, his show appealed to everyone. Men, women, college students, old, young, rich, poor. His phone lines were lit up every night from midnight to 2:00am with people who stayed up late to listen, and from 4:00am to 6:00am from people who got up early for work. From two to four, he played a lot of music. Good music. Different kinds of music from different eras.

He was number one in Dallas in his time slot by his second month on the job, but he never told Abbott and I that. The General Manager of KROQ in Los Angeles heard his show one night when he was in Dallas on business and bought the syndication rights.

"You're listening to The Greatest Mann in the World on 104.1, K-D-A-L in Dallas," John said over the airwaves. "Want to give a shout out to our listeners on K-R-O-Q in Los Angeles. Nick and Abbott, this song is for you..."

We were closing *The Shanty* some 2,000 miles away as Queen's "Another One Bites the Dust" played. A glass slipped out of a stunned Abbott's hand and shattered on the floor.

XIII
~THE MISTAKE BY THE LAKE~

Jim Carson was living proof you didn't have to be a good football player to be a good coach. He had been a backup quarterback on every team he played on from Pee-Wee to Midget to Pop Warner to high school. In fact, the only game he ever started was on Senior Day in high school, when his appearance consisted of three handoffs followed by a punt, before being replaced.

In college, he wasn't even good enough to be the backup, and had to settle for being the manager for legendary coach, Paul DelloStritto at Yale. But there was no questioning his football mind. He knew exactly how and why to advance the ball from point A to B—even if he wasn't physically capable of doing it himself. Paulie D, as he was referred to in coaching circles, saw something special in this self-motivated kid and named him a grad assistant upon his graduation. A couple of years later, he made him a full-time assistant in charge of the running backs. Little did both of them know at the time, but nine years down the road, a care-free running back from Connecticut would forever change both of their careers for the better.

Two All-American honors, four Ivy League Championships, and three Coach of the Year Awards later, and both Paulie D and Jim Carson were headed to the NFL's Cleveland Browns— Paulie as the Offensive Coordinator; Carson as the Running Backs coach. When DelloStritto finally retired from football at the ripe old age of 68, Carson was named the Offensive Coordinator under new coach, Steve Waller.

John had kept in touch with both of his former coaches on and off over the years, but had let about five years lapse between conversations, when he picked up the phone one early July morning to ask Jim Carson for a favor.

"Coach. It's John Mann."

"Johnnn Mannnnn." Carson said with equal parts surprise and admiration. "What's it been? Two, three years?"

"Probably closer to five actually."

"I thought you were dead, but then one night I decided to take a break from watching film by listening to the radio. And I heard this familiar voice speaking to me. This charlatan of a know-it-all who called himself 'The Greatest Mann in the World'. And I said to myself. *That* is John Freakin Mann."

"They syndicated my show in Cleveland?"

"Yes, and you were hammering Wally pretty good if I recall correctly."

Waller had always been a favorite target of his.

"Did he hear it?"

"You bet he did."

"Did you tell him you knew me?"

"I thought it better if I didn't."

"That's good to hear, especially in light of the favor I'm about to ask you."

"What do you need? Tickets for a few games?"

"I'm afraid it's a bit more involved than that," John answered. He was searching for the best way to present what he was about to ask, but decided the direct approach was the best. "I need you to get me a tryout with the Browns."

He waited a good two or three minutes for the laughter to subside on the other end of the phone. It had played out differently in his mind.

"You're joking obviously," Carson said.

"Not joking."

"Is it some radio stunt like when George Plimpton went through pre-season with the Lions?"

"Something like that." John wasn't allowed to tell him the truth.

"Wally will never go for it. He's way too strict and serious to put up with the media circus something like that would attract."

"What about if I didn't tell anyone about it until it was all over?"

"And how exactly am I supposed to sell it to him?"

"You always said I was the best running back you had ever coached."

"You were."

"And that I could have been a star at any Division I school in the country."

"You could have—15 years ago. How long's it been since you've played in an organized game?"

"About ten years," John admitted, "unless you count the alumni game at Yale five years ago. I scored three touchdowns."

"Against 50 year olds!"

"I still run a 4.34 forty."

That was cause for Carson to stop and think for a moment. If true, it would place John among the five fastest players in the league. Unfortunately, the league was littered with former track stars who couldn't hack it in the NFL.

"It's a different game now, John. You need to be smart enough to make lightening fast decisions; strong enough to take a hit from a 250 pound linebacker who is almost as fast as you; and durable enough to get back up after taking one of those hits."

"I understand that."

"Coaches have gotten fired for even joking about things like this."

"C'mon. You guys were 4-12 last year. Besides...you owe me." He hated doing it, but he was going to have to cash in his big chip.

Owe for which thing, Carson wondered.

"I introduced you to your wife, for heaven's sake," John said.

"I know you did. And now we have three kids, a dog and a mortgage, so I can't really afford to lose this job."

"She was my graduate teaching assistant," John continued, in case he needed a refresher course. "And when the school found out and wanted to fire you for dating a student, I stepped in and said I was the one dating her. You wouldn't have a job in coaching right now if it wasn't for me. Certainly not in the NFL."

All of which was true.

"Ok."

"Ok?"

"I'll get you a tryout, but I'm not going to promise you'll ever step on the field or even make the roster. In fact, I can pretty much promise you that you won't do either. When Wally asks, I'm going to tell him you played for us at Yale, and I saw you play over in Europe in some B division play for pizza league, and thought you were worth a quick look."

"That's fine."

"And no media coverage. I don't want this to end up on your radio show."

"It won't."

"After this, we're even."

"Unless I lead you to the playoffs," John smiled.

"I swear Mann, if you show up with a spare tire around your waist weighing 260 pounds, I'm going to tell security you're trespassing and have you thrown off the grounds immediately."

"I'm in the best shape of my life, coach."

That much was true. Every day, after he finished his show, he went for a timed three mile run, followed by two hours at the gym for agility and strength work with a personal trainer.

"Get your ass to Cleveland by the 20th," Carson said.

*   *   *

John didn't look at all out of place during the first week of camp. He was fit, quick and had always had good hands. And when he crossed the line in 4.32 seconds in the timed forty, he went from the unnoticed to the "keep a watchful eye on" list.

Most teams kept a total of five running backs on their roster—two, strictly for blocking, something that John was nowhere near big enough to do. That eliminated two spots. The Browns also returned the NFL's Rookie of the Year in Joe Campbell—the kid who led them to three consecutive wins to close out the previous season after a 1-12 start. His backup was a five year pro—a solid and durable runner from "The" Ohio State University. That left one spot open with six guys competing for it.

On one hand, John liked his chances. In addition to Carson, the Browns new GM, Michael Lombardi, had long liked the idea of making a name for himself by discovering "undiscovered" talent in his four previous stops.

The problem was that also competing for a spot was an unknown running back from Louisiana-Monroe who was seven years John's junior.

Three pre-season games came and went with John playing only on Special Teams, the unit players referred to as the "players no one cares if they get hurt" unit. He had two tackles and busted up one wedge in efforts that went largely unnoticed. But in the final game, he actually carried the ball three times; one for 17 yards and another for six, before fumbling his third carry and then pulling his arms back on a pass play when the quarterback threw the ball high over the middle, because he was afraid of getting hit. He got flattened anyway. Lesson learned.

"You ever see The 40 Year Old Virgin?" his roommate asked that night. Jimbo Evans was a Notre Dame boy, and a four-time All-Pro Offensive Guard. He and John ended up roommates as part of Wally's desire to match up running backs and quarterbacks with their linemen.

"Of course," John said.

"Well, they should make a movie about you called 'The 33 year old Pussy'. If you weren't so afraid of getting hit, you might actually have a shot at making this team."

"Thanks. I think."

"It's true. You hit the holes quicker than any of the other backs. You can catch the ball. But damn if you aren't a pussy."

It was the last and most difficult part of the game to get back. Strategically, the west coast spread offense that most NFL teams ran was actually easier on running backs, because most of the burden fell on the quarterback and wide receivers. When they did run, the defense was so spread out, it was easier to find the openings. And he still was lightning fast. His problem was that while he had never enjoyed getting hit, he had usually been able to avoid what was referred to as "bad" contact, by his ability to stop on a dime and change direction. Now he was like an old muscle car. He could accelerate just fine, but his brakes were shot. And unlike a car, which could replace worn pads and rotors, humans had no such solution.

There was a knock on the door. The running back coach stuck his head in. He was gruff, grey and perpetually pissed off. "Carson wants to see you," the man told John.

"Let me start by saying that you have been infinitely more impressive than I thought you would be in my wildest dreams," Carson began. "How, is beyond my comprehension. Having said that, as you know, we basically have six backs competing for one spot. You're the oldest one by three years, which is like 20 in NFL years. Now, I don't know what the real reason for all this is. Maybe it's a publicity stunt. Maybe you're having a mid-life crisis. Maybe you're trying to impress some girl. And quite frankly, I don't really want to know. Someday, when it's all over, you can explain it to me. But for now, I'm going to listen to what Jimbo had to say and make you our number three back."

"You mean I'm on??"

"You're on. But I wouldn't get too excited about it. Number three backs almost never see the field. If the number one or two goes down, the club will usually trade for another number two. Probably the only chance you have of seeing the field is if both guys go down on the same day, and even then, my guess is we'd play with just a blocking back and three wide receivers."

"I understand."

"You also have to prepare yourself for the reality that you could get cut, if Wally and Lombardi decide we need to pick up another receiver or tight end."

"Got it. But for now, I'm on."

"For now you are. Congratulations."

"Can I ask you what Jimbo said?"

"He said 'smart and fast is better than strong and stupid', and if he had to block for one of the six guys trying out, he'd feel most comfortable if it was you—even if you are a bit of a pussy.'"

John nodded. That sounded about right. "Thanks, coach."

"How'd it go?" Jimbo asked.

"I guess I need to start looking for an apartment in Cleveland," John answered. "And from what I understand, I have you to thank for it."

"It was nothing. Besides, I'm tired of blocking for idiots. I thought it was about time we had some intelligence on this team."

"I never thought I'd ever be living in Cleveland. The mistake by the lake," John lamented.

"No one ever does, buddy. But it grows on you after a while."

XIV
~GOD, FATE AND A
BOTTLE OF TEQUILA~

John had heard about big time football players' feelings of invincibility and superiority, but had experienced it previously only one time before that moment. He had been vacationing in South Beach with some friends when a couple of Miami Dolphins decided to pick a fight with them. Fortunately, a friend of a friend was an Italian guy who ran a "refrigeration" company in Boston, and after a brief exchange between Johnny Carbone and the manager of the club, the reserve linebackers soon found themselves in the same position they usually were on Sunday afternoons—on the outside looking in.

He had heard of similar instances from his friends at big time college programs, but had never experienced it firsthand. At Yale, football players fell slightly below the President of the Young Republicans and Editor of the Student Newspaper on the popularity chart, mainly because most of the students resented the fact that the majority of them would never have been admitted were it not for football. Ranked number one in his class with near perfect SATs, John was the exception to the rule, but had still never found himself the beneficiary of being handed the answers to a midterm two days before the test, or the keys to a loaner SUV for a weekend getaway, much less have beautiful co-eds throw themselves at him at any party he happened to walk into. That was reserved for players from the big time, Top 20 programs of the world. Hand them 30 million dollars after graduation and one imagined their attitude wouldn't improve much.

This time, John was in a club in Cleveland—amazed that there *were* clubs in Cleveland—with about ten members of the Browns. It was his first inside glance at their very public, private lives. He supposed there were plusses and minuses to any lifestyle. On the plus side, they didn't ever have to wait in line to get into a place. They also rarely were asked to pay for drinks, even though they could have paid for drinks for everyone in the bar ten times over with a day's pay. The negative was that five minutes also rarely passed without someone shoving a piece of paper, napkin, t-shirt, or bra in their face to sign, conversations were almost never private, and heaven forbid they were in a bad mood or simply not feeling well and snapped at someone; because it usually ended up in the newspaper the following morning. But he also supposed six million dollars a year was a fair price for the inconveniences—a tradeoff that any American not named Gates, Buffet, Bush, Obama or the lead singer of any rock band, would probably take in an instant.

Two average Joes were having fun playing pool with their girlfriends, when a couple of the Browns decided the girls were far too cute to be with these guys and moved in. The poor guys had limited choices. Stand up for themselves and get their asses kicked. Or back down and be embarrassed in front of their girls. John was watching it all unfold about twenty feet away when he decided he couldn't just stand by and let it happen.

"Darrell. Ray," he said as he approached. "Jimbo and I are throwing down the gauntlet—if you think you guys are man enough to handle it. One bottle of Grey Goose. Team shot contest. First one to puke loses."

Jimbo knew what John was up to, and backed him up, holding a bottle of Vodka up as incentive. The other two thought it over for an uncomfortable couple of seconds before leaving the pool players alone. John could see one of the players let out a visible sigh of relief, and he winked at him, mouthing the word, "Sorry" as he walked past.

"You're not going to be a very popular rookie if you keep interfering in the veterans' business," Jimbo warned.

"I know, but I couldn't stand by and do nothing. Those guys weren't bothering anyone. They were just out for a night with their girls."

It made sense to Jimbo. It was just easy to forget that from time to time.

The next thing John remembered was opening his eyes one at a time in his bedroom at Jimbo's house, where he had been living for the past three weeks. The curtains were closed, but the television was on. His right arm was wrapped gently around a beautiful, half-naked woman he didn't recognize, while she rested her head on his chest with her right leg wrapped around his. In his left hand, pointed firmly at the television, was the remote control, poised for a channel change that apparently never happened.

His stirring seemed to wake her as well. "Good morning," she said with a smile.

"Morning," he responded curiously.

"You don't have any idea who I am, do you?"

"Sure I do," he said unconvincingly.

"We met at Big Al's."

"Erin," he said, his memory slowly coming back to him.

"What's the last thing you remember?"

"I remember being in a shot contest with Jimbo, Darrell and Ray."

"That's when we met."

"Did Jimbo and I win?"

"That depends on your definition of winning. They threw up first, but as you stood up to celebrate, you lost your balance and fell backward into a table full of people."

"But we won."

"Yes, it was very impressive."

"Then what happened?"

"A brawl broke out, the bouncers pushed us all out the back door, and we came back here where you made me watch some terrible B movie on USA called, 'Big Bad Mama' before we both passed out."

"That's a classic. So that's it?" he asked, scanning her tone, curvy body with regret at either not having done anything or not remembering it if he did.

"We both have some clothes on, so it would appear to be."

"Did I say anything stupid?"

"Just something about you not really being a pro football player and being a girls high school basketball coach instead."

"Wow. I must have really been out of it."

"You were very sweet. Not like the other guys. But I have to go to class," she said.

"Class?"

"I go to Carnegie Melon."

"You're in *college?*"

"Sophomore year."

"Oh geez," he mumbled. "Need a ride?"

"I drove *you* home," she winked.

"That's probably a good thing."

"Call me," she said, as she kissed him on the cheek.

Jimbo downed a huge glass of orange juice as

if he hadn't had a drink in days, which was interesting because he had about 20 the previous evening. "How was she?"

"I wouldn't know," John answered.

"What do you mean you wouldn't know?"

"I mean, I wouldn't know even if I did, which I apparently didn't."

"Passed out, huh?"

"Cold. How about you?"

"I...was a true Wingman last night. I jumped on the grenade."

"I'm sure it was not without reason."

"I did go to Notre Dame. Mathematically, I figured there was a greater chance of the ugly one putting out."

"And how'd that work out for ya?"

"Not so much. Apparently, my calculations were off. You better get ready. Film session starts at 1."

Afternoon sessions of any kind were the biggest adjustment for someone who was used to sleeping all afternoon, so he could stay up all night on the radio. Throw in a dark room, and a droning, monotonous voice talking about blocking schemes, and John was usually asleep within minutes. It was a decision he would come to regret Sunday afternoon.

Sunday mornings at *The Shanty*--when you factored in the three hour time difference from the East Coast--had become quite a happening, as people packed the place to watch the Browns' games on the satellite dish. To a casual observer who happened in off the street, the phenomenon of why so many Los Angeles residents were such fans of the Cleveland Browns, didn't make much sense, but it wasn't long before every transplanted Clevelandite or long-time Browns fan found their way down to Hermosa Beach.

For the first seven weeks of the season, most fans went home disappointed, as number 33 never stepped on the field, although the camera did catch him one time standing near the coaches during a timeout. But in week seven, God intervened—with a little help from a bottle of tequila.

The Browns second string running back, upset over a lack of carries in the first seven games, decided to stay out most of the night and didn't arrive at the stadium until the second quarter, in no condition to play, at which point the coaches were so pissed off, they suspended him on the spot and sent him home. In the third quarter, with the Browns trailing 14-3, Joe Campbell, tore up his knee trying to get an extra yard, and was carted from the field.

After two offensive series where the Browns tried unsuccessfully to play with just one blocking back and three wide receivers, the person whose nickname in college was "The Greatest Mann in the World" jogged onto the field. You could almost *hear* the Browns fans shuffling through their game programs trying to find out who he was.

His first play left John wishing he had stayed awake for a few of the film sessions as two Dallas Cowboys came running at him towards his otherwise unprotected quarterback. Needing to make a split second decision, he dove at the legs of the inside rusher, taking him to the ground a mere inches from the quarterback's face. The other one arrived a second later, but the ball was already gone for a 12 yard completion. Unfortunately, John's block was what was also called a "clip" and the Browns were penalized 15 yards for it. Personally, he thought he had saved his quarterback's life, but he didn't seem to be receiving much gratitude for it.

On his second play, he was supposed to let the defenders through and immediately release into the flat as a last ditch outlet. With three defensive linemen in his face, the Browns QB tossed the ball in a panic in John's general direction. Instinctively, he reached out and snared the ball with his left hand, while tossing a would-be tackler away with his right, and headed up field. John felt like he was in the middle of a video game, with big, fast, strong men coming at him from every direction. He shook another tackler at the 25, let one fly past him at the 30, and spun away from the outstretched arms of a third at the 33, before he headed for the sideline. His goal was to get safely out of bounds, and he was running as fast as his legs would take him. But as he turned the corner, he realized he had nothing but open field in front of him. There also were only three players in the league faster than him and none of them played for the Cowboys.

Fifty yards later, he was in the end zone and in his excitement, threw the ball up into the upper deck of the stadium. It was an impressive toss of at least sixty yards.

When John bulldozed into the end zone a second time, with only a minute remaining in the game to give the Browns a 17-14 victory, Browns Stadium was whipped into a frenzy, just as a man-made 7.1 sized earthquake shook the small bar located at 13201 The Strand in Hermosa Beach. Even people who had bet against him were celebrating their friend now. Hugging. Jumping up and down. Screaming. Throwing things into the air. Abbott high fived me as he grabbed a green marker and walked to the eraser board. He placed a big checkmark, with a smile to match, on the board next to the words *Pro Football Player* and then threw the marker into the cheering crowd.

The Browns, for only the third time since they re-started football operations in 1999, were in a playoff race.

Meanwhile, at K D A L radio, the official station of the Dallas Cowboys, Station Manager, Scott McBride, casually listened to the game over the loud speakers while he caught up on some paperwork in an otherwise empty station. He paused for the briefest of moments at the announcer's mention of the name, John Mann, before continuing to work. The man who had been "The Greatest Mann in the World" in Dallas, was now "The Greatest Mann in the World" in Cleveland, but never in a million years did McBride think it was the *same* man, who was supposedly off "tending to family business".

Meanwhile, four hundred miles away from Cleveland in Salisbury, Connecticut, football was the last thing on the mind of Joe Kovac as he sat down to watch a DVR episode of "Meet the Press". But two blocks over, Tom Hubbard was watching the nationally televised game.

"Sonuvabitch," he grinned as he took a sip of his beer.

Across town, at that very moment, Melissa Baldwin glanced up at the television while having brunch with her parents, just in time to see John Mann's face flash across the screen. She nearly choked on her pancakes.

XV
˜THE GREATEST MAN IN THE WORLD˜

The pain John felt the day after playing a football game at twenty-two years of age couldn't compare with the pain he felt the day after playing a football game at age thirty-three, any more than the pain of getting hit by a 195 pound future chemist could compare to the pain of getting hit by a 250 pound wrecking machine. Every joint and muscle in his body ached. His head throbbed. And his neck felt as if half the tendons that kept it attached to the rest of his body had been shredded. The amazing thing being that he had only carried the ball six times and caught two passes the entire game.

"Jimbo, tell me it gets easier as the season continues," he said, delicately dragging himself into the kitchen.

"I could tell you that, buddy, but it just wouldn't be true," Jimbo responded. "There's a reason Jim Brown retired when he was thirty years old."

Jim Brown was a Cleveland running back in the late fifties and early sixties, widely considered to be the greatest NFL back of all time. He held the all-time league rushing mark for more than 20 years, despite only playing for nine seasons during a time when there were 14 games in a season, instead of the 16 they played now.

"I thought he retired because he wanted to act?"

"If someone offered you similar money without getting hit all day long, you would do it too."

Jimbo had a valid point, and it made John suddenly long for the days where he was paid the same amount for doing little more than warm the bench on the sideline.

"I don't know how much punishment this old body can handle," John said.

"You better suck it up. You're all we've got right now."

"Gee, you make it sound like such a compliment when you phrase it like that."

"C'mon. You're The Greatest Mann in the World!" Jimbo said as he tossed the sports section to him with that very heading.

He had already been the Savior of St. Francis and now he was The Greatest Mann in the World, but he wondered for how long. The answer to that question was at least five weeks, which was approximately the amount of time Campbell would be out. What was originally thought to be an ACL tear, turned out to be an MCL sprain. The timing couldn't have been better as far as John was concerned. By that time, he would have been in Cleveland for more than five months and running out of time to move on to the next job. And even though being a professional athlete certainly had its benefits, a bet was a bet. Besides, John had no intention of being one of those players who spent their declining years in a wheel chair or walking with a permanent limp.

The wrinkle that developed, was that the Browns went 4-1 during that span, needing only one more victory to clinch a playoff spot that had seemed so remote when the season began. John was a large part of the success, having averaged more than 100 yards a game with single game highs of 26 carries for 202 yards against the defending AFC Champion Steelers. Because of that fact, both the coaching staff and the players were reluctant to mess with a winning formula.

"The line has been blowing open holes big enough for a dump truck to drive through," John said.

"If a team thinks it's winning because a certain player is playing, then it is," Jim Carson explained in answer to John's question of whether he could be removed from the starting lineup with Campbell coming back. "You don't mess with a winning streak, John. Don't forget how Tom Brady got his big break."

Brady, the New England Patriots star quarterback had been a backup to longtime Patriot QB, Drew Bledsoe. Bledsoe got hurt, Brady excelled and Bledsoe ended up being traded while Brady won three Super Bowls.

It was becoming apparent that the only way he would be removed from the lineup—short of purposely playing horribly—would be if he took care of it himself. The only two people that were privy to the plan had flown all night from California on the red eye. Abbott and I took our seats in the family and friends section, behind the team bench near midfield. The Browns were hosting the Cincinnati Bengals during week 14, with playoff implications for both teams on the line.

The game began as each of the past five had, with John ripping off a few solid gains as the Browns moved down the field. But a third down pass reception across the middle left him exposed. When John went down from a hard hit and didn't get up, the only sound that could be heard in the stadium was the wind howling off of Lake Erie. The trainers and doctors rushed to his side and found him breathing, but seemingly unconscious. If smelling salts could wake the unconscious, waving them under the nose of someone who was actually conscious was almost enough to cause him to pass out. As they helped him to his feet, Abbott and I took our cue and headed for the exit.

A concussion was the one injury John knew would not necessarily show up in a CT scan or MRI, and he had taken enough Impact tests over the years to know how to fail one. They took him to the hospital as a precaution and Abbott and I met him there. We waited for John's text as to which room he was in and waited for the nurse to leave the room before entering.

"Browns are down seven. Campbell has minus 5 yards rushing. Sure you don't want to go back?" I asked as I tossed John a change of clothes and a baseball cap.

"I'm afraid I have a prior engagement. After all, a bet—"

"—is a bet. Yes, I know."

"Campbell will be fine. The bye next week will give him two more weeks to get back to 100%. They only need to win one of the last two if they lose today."

John had always claimed to have a generic looking face; people were always saying hello and talking to him thinking they knew him when they didn't. Sometimes they thought he was someone famous. Other times they thought he was the cousin of a friend. Without his jersey on, he magically looked liked no one in particular and everyone all at the same time. We walked right out the front door of the emergency room without so much as a second look. As we did, I tried to picture the nurse returning to the room where she had left the The Greatest Mann in the World, only to find nothing but a brown #33 jersey pulled tightly over a set of shoulder pads, along with a pair of muddied orange football pants laying straight out in front of them. I pictured the Wicked Witch of the West in *The Wizard of Oz* after she had melted away, and it made me smile just thinking about it.

XVI
~WHAT HAPPENS IN VEGAS...~

John felt the beady eyes come up over his shoulder as he read. Out of the many inconveniences of flying, and there were many—long lines, disrobing for security, having to check a bag because you couldn't bring more than a spoonful of toiletry items onboard—John hated sitting next to someone he didn't know for a cross country flight more than any of them. Southwest Airlines was cheap, usually on time, and flew directly into Las Vegas, but they didn't assign seats, so John, Abbott and I found ourselves separated by a few rows each.

During the five hour flight, in order to avoid conversation, John had feigned sleep, listened to his IPod until the battery died, and read a magazine before deciding to do a little research for his next occupation by reading up on card counting.

"If card counting worked, everyone would do it," the man seated next to him said.

Not everyone has an adding machine for a mind, John thought, but answered with, "I know. I just find the mathematics of it interesting."

"Are you a Mathematician or scientist?"

The man was short, fat, and bald, with a mustache and enough hair coming out of his ears and nose to look like a party favor.

"Nope. Just have always been interested in numbers."

And he had read all the books. *Bringing Down the House*. *Blackjack for Dummies*. *Card Counting Made Easy*. *How to Count Cards and Beat the Casino*. The basic premise of counting cards was to have a calculated guess as to when the higher cards might be coming out. Higher cards meant a greater chance of getting Blackjack and also a greater chance of the dealer breaking. It wasn't a guarantee of winning. It was just a way over the long haul of tilting a game your way that was 51 to 49 in the casino's favor. John's plan was to formulate his own system using the best ideas from each.

"Even if you could count cards, which very few people can, the casino has developed ways to counteract it. Fast dealers. Shuffle machines. Cutting into the shoe. Single decks with the cards face down. You can't beat them," the man continued.

"Can I ask why you're going to Vegas then?"

"To play the only game where a good player can actually win. The World Series of Poker is in town at Harrah's starting next week. I'm going to make a little money playing cash games first and then play in the main event."

"Well, good luck to you," John said, really

hoping it would be the last of the conversation.

"You don't need luck in poker. You need to be good."

"What happens when you are getting lousy cards?"

"You make people think you have good ones," the man countered.

"Hope that works out for ya," John said as the lights on the strip became visable in the not so far off distance.

It was a little after 9:00pm on a Sunday by the time the three of us checked into our suite at Caesar's Palace. The casino was certainly showing no signs of a recession.

"Nice room!" Abbott remarked.

"If you want to be the best, you have to act like you're the best. I told them I'd be here for a month and planned on gambling an obscene amount of money over that time, so they set me up in this suite."

A wall-to-wall window with a panoramic view of the strip lined one side of the room, while two couches, a 50 inch flat screen TV and a baby grand piano decorated it. There were three bedrooms, each larger than his entire apartment back in Hermosa Beach, along with a bathroom with marble countertops, three individual basins, a Jacuzzi and both a telephone and television.

I remembered thinking that I would have rented just the bathroom and comfortably slept in the Jacuzzi. It was far and away the nicest hotel room I had seen in Vegas, or anywhere else for that matter. My last sojourn to Vegas consisted of arriving late on a Friday night after a four and a half hour drive across the desert, followed by a 12 to 14 hour gambling shift during which I consumed at least as many Moosehead lagers. We used our room at the Raccoon Lodge only to store our bags and shower. At least it had been cheap.

Out of four of us, I was the only one who ended up making any money which, in the unwritten rules of gambling, meant that I was required to pay for breakfast and the gas to get home. Somewhere in the middle of the desert, the air conditioner on my friend's new BMW crapped out in the 110 degree heat and I ended up sweating out beer and moaning in agony for the better part of three hours. Hopefully, this trip would work out better.

"So, what are you going to play first?" Abbott asked.

"I'm going to play the only games in the casino you actually have a chance to win at. Blackjack. Poker. And Roulette."

"Roulette?!"

"Gather round, gentlemen. School is in session," John answered. "Roulette is the game that's going to pay for this room."

"How so?" I asked, curious.

"It's the one game where you can bet large amounts, but cover your bets so you don't actually *lose* a lot on each spin. Sometimes you win, sometimes you lose, but you can play for hours at $300 a spin, with minimal losses. All the pit boss sees is that you're playing $300 a spin. They don't have time to analyze everyone's bets. The result is that you get a ton of comp points, hence, the room paid for."

"Brilliant. But how are you going to *make* money for certain? To be a successful gambler, you need to actually make money," Abbott said. "Any clown can get a room paid for if he's pissed away enough money."

"The money making will be done at the blackjack and poker tables."

"You know how to count cards?" I asked.

He removed a fresh deck from his pocket and began dealing the cards face up on the coffee table. "Everyone counts cards a little differently. Some count Aces as high cards. Some count them as low. Others have a separate count for them altogether. The MIT guys considered 10's, Jack's, Queen's, King's and Ace's as high cards. 2 through 6 as low. And 7, 8 and 9 as neutral cards. Granted, they were very successful, but they had to be patient enough to wait for a good count. The other problem with their system was the neutral cards. 7, 8 and 9 don't seem very neutral when you're sitting on a 14, 15 or 16 against the dealer's face card. You could have a pretty good idea that low cards were coming, but if one of your neutral cards hit instead, you'd break. I consider 8, 9, 10 and the three face cards as high. Ace's through 6 as low and only 7 as neutral. It minimizes the effect of the neutral cards. Do you follow me?'

"I don't follow you in the slightest," Abbott said, his head visibly spinning now.

"I follow you," I said. "If you had a 13, 14 or 15 and thought low cards were coming out, you could hit your hand reasonably comfortably. But what about if high cards were coming?"

"You use a very underrated and underused play called a surrender."

"I thought you were never supposed to surrender."

"That's what the dealers want you to think. But answer me this. If it was such a bad play by the player, why do only three casinos on the entire strip allow you to do it?"

He had a point. If you were sitting on a dead hand, far better to give up half your bet than to lose all of it.

"Card counting is all about knowing when to surrender and when to bet big. You do the first when the odds are against you. You do the second, when the odds are in your favor. Keep in mind, card counting doesn't guarantee success. You could be a psychic and know precisely what card is due to come out next and you could still lose the hand if you have a 16 and the next card is a 7 and the dealer already has a 20. You're playing for the long haul with the hope that over time, you win. The thing you have to prepare for is people going crazy at the table when you do something unusual. The book players get pissed. They also lose 51% of the time."

"I repeat. You know how to count cards?" I asked again.

"I use a method I call up and down the river. I look at the first card out. If it's a high card, I count all the high cards first. In the hand I just dealt, there are five of them. Each worth +1. So that's +5. Then I work backwards with the low cards. For every low card, I subtract a point. +4, +3, +2. I ignore the 7's. Done. The count is +2. What you're looking for is a situation where the count is -10 with only a deck and a half left in the shoe. That's when you really up your bet."

"I understand."

"I don't understand a thing. Can we go gamble now and look at some chicks?" Abbott said.

The interesting thing about Vegas was that with legalized prostitution, it was sometimes difficult to tell the pros from the amateurs. Similarly, it was also difficult to tell the married women from the single ones because they all acted single.

Standing over by one of the roulette tables was a brunette with long, wavy hair. She was pretty in a high-maintenance sort of way. It was unlikely you would ever see her in a pair of jeans and a sweatshirt, and that seemed ok with all the men in the room. The women, if asked, would have immediately described her as "trashy", less because she was, than because that was their response whenever there was a woman men found sexy. Her form fitting black dress did nothing to disguise her well put together figure. Her chest, if it was real, was nothing short of spectacular. If it wasn't, well, I doubted anyone would complain much. She could have been a pro. She could have been married. It made no difference to Abbott.

"Hey, there," he began, "how'd you like a pizza and a—"

I drilled him in the chest with a well-placed elbow, succeeding in cutting him off mid-sentence and also winding him in the process.

"What the hell?" he gasped. "I was going to say pizza and a beer!"

"Oh, I love Italian food," the woman cooed in a little girl voice that suggested her IQ might actually be lower than her three inch heels.

"Beautiful," Abbott said, holding his arm out to escort her away. She apparently wasn't that high maintenance after all.

I learned two things at that moment. One. Don't judge a book by its cover. And two. Even Abbott could get laid in Vegas.

"Can we get down to business now?" John asked.

"Absolutely," I answered as we bellied up to the table.

"Here's the beauty of my system. There isn't a lot of memorization involved which means you can play it if you're the only one at the table or if there are 15 people cramming in. The key to roulette is to stay alive long enough to hit your numbers. The way you do that is by covering your bet."

His system was indeed simple enough. He sprayed 17 ten dollar chips among the 26 numbers on the top part of the board. He then played $85 on the back third. If a number came in the back third, he broke even to the penny. If he hit one of his numbers, and there was nearly a 70% chance of that happening, he made $105.

If he missed entirely, he lost $255.

Watching John play roulette was a little like examining the stock market. He would go up a little, then down a little. Occasionally, he would miss a couple in a row, but then he would hit four or five in a row. Overall, like the market in a non-recession era, he was up. More importantly, the pit boss only saw him as someone playing $255 a spin, not really paying attention to the fact that it would be extremely difficult to lose (or make for that matter) a ton of money playing that way.

It always made me laugh when some guy would come up with his last $50 and put it all on one number, and then act genuinely shocked when it didn't come in. The odds were only 1 in 38. What did he really expect to happen? Or the person who would be lucky enough to hit one of their magic numbers, make almost a grand, and then piss it all away a few spins of the wheel later. There was even one person who bet on *both* red and black.

John and I walked away from the table two

hours later up $680 with about $300 worth of comp points. Abbott finally rejoined us at the blackjack tables.

"Well?" John asked.

"Well what?"

"Was she a pro?"

"If she was, she must be into *pro bono* work, if you get what I'm saying," he replied with a wink.

"Don't confuse the fact that most people find the things you say stupid, with them not understanding you," John answered, before adding, "And are you sure you don't mean *pro boner* work?"

"I like that!" Abbott laughed. "I'm going to have to use it."

"It would be better if you didn't encourage him," I said as they high-fived.

John sat in the first seat at the table. When you were pretty sure high cards were coming, you wanted to make sure you got the first crack at them. A Chinese woman in her 50's sat next to him. She didn't appear to speak much English. Kobe Bryant, or possibly someone wearing Kobe Bryant's Laker jersey—it was kind of tough to tell--sat next to her. He was an overweight, white man with a flat-brimmed Nike baseball cap and two-day old beard growth with the mustache part shaved, sporting oversized jeans barely covering his stained boxer shorts. He could have been Kobe's doppelganger, although it's doubtful Kobe would have agreed. Next up was Mr.

Blackjack. The guy who played by the book, and got upset whenever others didn't. He sported a fake Rolex, along with a Polo knock-off and pair of Dockers. One thing was certain. He was going to hate playing with John. Finally, there was an older gentleman. Distinguished looking. Friendly. Well-spoken, but it appeared, sadly, alone. I stood in the background, attempting to master the art of card-counting, but losing track every couple of hands whenever someone started talking to me or an attractive woman stilettoed by.

The first hour or so was relatively event-free. John stayed on an occasional 16 and surrendered a few hands some people would have played, but otherwise he mostly followed the book. He was up $60 after the first shoe, then $85 after the second, then back to even after the third, when things suddenly got interesting about halfway through the fourth.

After betting $25-$35 for most of the time, John suddenly tossed eight green chips onto the table and received an Ace and 9, for a twenty against the dealer's 6.

"Happy Days!" I thought to myself. That should be a cool $200.

But then John tossed eight more green chips onto the table. "Double down," he said, to everyone's shock.

"You have a 20," the dealer said.

"Or a 10," John responded.

"Are you an idiot?!" Mr. Blackjack

screamed. "Never break up a 20!"

"If you had a 6 and 4 against the dealer's break card, would you double down?" John asked, calmly.

"Yes, but this is different," the man said, getting irritated and not feeling as comfortable with his 17. "You never break up a winning hand."

"Gambling is all about getting more of your money on the table when the odds are right. The odds, in my mind, are right."

"It's his money, let him piss it away if he wants," Kobe interjected, as he pulled back the winnings from his blackjack.

"Gentlemen. We have no way of knowing what the next card will be. Maybe it will be a five. Or maybe the dealer has a ten under there and that five would give him 21. The only thing we know for certain is that there is a card about to come out, and I for one, wish my friend luck with his $400," the older gentleman said.

"Thank you," John nodded.

The next card out was a Queen, giving John a 20—again. He winked at me when it hit the table. The Chinese woman stayed on a 15. Mr. Blackjack stayed nervously on his 17. The gentleman stayed on 19. The dealer turned over another 6 for a 12, then hit. He pulled a third 6 for an 18. The Chinese woman muttered some unintelligible gibberish and stormed away. Mr. Blackjack pounded the table in frustration. "You asshole!" he screamed. The old man smiled as collected his $30 and John let out an audible sigh of relief as he was handed four black chips for his efforts.

"If you had just stayed like you were supposed to, the dealer would have broke!" Mr. Blackjack continued.

The ranting would continue for quite some time, until John stayed on a 15 against the dealer's King, and the dealer turned over a five and then broke with the next card.

"He saved the table by staying," the gentleman said. "If he had hit, he would have broke, you would have gotten my 6 and then broke. And I would have had a 17."

"That all depends on the next card," Mr. Blackjack grumbled.

The next card was a 6.

"My name is Andy," the gentleman said, reaching across to shake John's hand.

"Nice to meet you, Andy. I'm John. And you're welcome," he said with a sideways glance at Mr. Blackjack, who ignored him.

John then proceeded to go on a run like I've never seen. He didn't win every hand, but he did win most of them, and it seemed as though the ones he did, were the ones he had the most money on. Thirty-seven hundred dollars later, he decided to call it an evening. It was 3:00am.

"Want to get a late-night munch?" he asked.

"Definitely. I was about to eat my shirt," I said.

"Thank god," Mr. Blackjack groused. He

was down a couple of grand at that point. "Maybe now someone will sit down who actually knows how to play."

"Hey, Captain Blackjack," Abbott interjected. "He knows how to play, to the tune of four grand, pal. You could have bought a real Rolex with all the money you've lost tonight. Idiot."

"You're so ignorant," the man said.

"I'm ignorant? I'm not the one following the rules of a book that is designed so the casino wins 51% of the time. Tell you what. You give me ten bucks and I'll give you $9.80 back. Then let's do it a couple of hundred times and see who has more money. Moron."

John shot me a pleased and surprised look at Abbott's response. Until then, he wasn't even sure he could add.

XVII
~THE REVERSE VIRGIN~

John had some housekeeping to take care of when he woke up in the morning. The Browns had lost and all of Cleveland wondered where its former 3rd string running back turned starter had gone.

"I went home," he explained to Jim Carson over the phone.

"Home being where? Dallas?"

"Yeah. Dallas."

"Why'd you just walk out of the hospital? Everyone went crazy looking for you."

"Sorry about that. There was a bad car crash and the doctors were all tied up. I got tired of waiting around."

"You left your uniform and pads in the room. Did you walk out of the hospital naked?"

"My buddy has a Smart car. He didn't have any room in it. He brought me a change of clothes." John cringed. Even he knew how ridiculous that all sounded.

"Smart car, huh? So how are you feeling anyway?"

"A little better. Still have a bit of a headache, but not too bad."

"When are you coming back?"

"The doctor here says I'm probably done for the season. He's worried about post-concussion syndrome."

"That's not good," Carson said. "You know the game went downhill after you got hurt."

"You guys will be fine with Campbell."

"Campbell sucked yesterday."

"He's just rusty. But with two weeks of practice before the next game, he'll be fine."

"You still should be back here. You're a part of the team. Plus, Wally will want you looked at by our doctors."

"I'll be back in a week or so," John said.

He hated lying to his old coach, knowing that he wouldn't be coming back. He would explain it all to him one day when it was over.

"What do you want me to tell Wally?"

"Tell him 'good luck'," John answered.

"By the way, this guy keeps calling for you at the stadium."

"What guy?"

"Some guy named Hubbard. Says he's a friend of yours."

"He is."

"I figured any real friend would have your cell phone number, which is what I told him."

"What did he say to that?"

"He said, and I quote, 'I do have his cell number you goofy bastard, but he hasn't been answering it, so I thought he might have changed it.'"

Good old Hubbard.

"He left a number. You want it?"

"That's ok. I've got it. And coach?"

"Yeah?"

"Thanks for everything."

Jim Carson knew at that very moment that John had no intention of returning.

"You take care of yourself, Mann."

His next call was to Scott McBride down in Dallas. McBride was someone who would have been just as comfortable on a ski slope or beach as he was a Station Manager. He was as laid back as they came. When John initially told him he was leaving for a family emergency, he responded with simply, "No worries." When he then called to thank him for the opportunity and tell him he wouldn't be returning, McBride told him once again not to worry. Not because he didn't like him or think he was talented, but because life was too short to worry over the little things. If the station tanked and McBride lost his job, he would simply find another one. It was a simple and probably healthy way to go through life. Besides, Christine had picked out John's replacement two days after he left.

He should have placed two more calls; one to Hubbard and one to Melissa, but he couldn't bring himself to call either. Hubbard because he knew he would end up telling him everything.

And Melissa because he didn't think it would matter to her if he did.

By the time we left on Sunday afternoon, John had already amassed more than $12,000. The ground rules were simple. Together, we opened a joint checking and savings account in Vegas. He deposited $10,000 in the checking account. At the end of the month, he needed to have made a livable wage for the month-- something in the neighborhood of $6,000 would do the trick--to win and move on to his last job. If he lost the ten grand during the month, he lost and the bet was over.

We left him with only his driver's license and a card to access that account, but took all of his other credit cards with us. We supposed he could have made a couple of calls and accessed his other accounts, but it wouldn't make much sense to spend $30,000 in hope of making $50,000. Besides, Abbott and I both knew John to be the most honest person we knew. Not to mention the fact that, unless he bet like an idiot, there was no way he could lose now. He was already up 12 grand. But he had to stay the full month nonetheless.

"We'll see you in a few weeks," I told him.

"Maybe sooner if you screw up," Abbott smirked.

He gave us both man hugs and sent us on our way. For the first time, John found himself feeling pretty much alone. No family. No friends. No roommates. He finally understood what his new friend from the blackjack table must have felt like.

Andy, as we had guessed, was indeed alone. A widower, whose wife had passed away three years ago from Cancer. He had grown up outside of New York City, but lived in Los Angeles now, finding it much more tolerable weather since his blood had thinned with age. He had two adult, married children, both living on the East Coast, that he saw three to four times a year. He had amassed a tidy sum as the owner of a small company that sold paper towel dispensers to other companies, but when neither child expressed an interest in taking over the family business, he sold it and retired.

Andy gave a good portion from the sale of his company to his kids so they could each buy a house and start married life as debt free as possible, and had spent another large chunk on medical bills for his wife. And yet, he could still live comfortably the remainder of his life, unless he lived past 117, at which point he might have to tighten the belt a little. He was in Vegas for a two week stretch, something he did two to three times a year, and John wondered if, considering his age, maybe it was because of the legalized prostitution thing. Andy assured him it wasn't.

"The day I start paying for sex," he laughed heartily, "is the day I should cut it off. Besides, sex isn't that much of a draw when you've already met and lost the love of your life. Sure, there are some women I find attractive, and even some I find sexy, but I know that if I ever ended up in bed with them, it would feel completely wrong."

"So you're like a reverse virgin," John stated, to hysterical laughter from his friend.

"Something like that," he smiled.

John couldn't help but feel sad and jealous at the same time. After all, how many people really found their soul mates? With a more than 50% divorce rate and another 70% of the ones that made it, tolerating marriage more than anything, not many, he figured.

The truth was, Andy came to Vegas because it was a place that allowed him to meet all sorts of interesting people from all walks of life. He was a former Army man, who had fought in parts of both Korea and Vietnam and could still make a bed so tight you could bounce a quarter off of it. His Vegas trips were regimented to the point where you could set your clock by them. Gambling until noon. Poolside until 4:00pm, followed by a shower and nice meal. Then people watching until 7:00 or so at various favorite spots of his, followed by more gambling until midnight.

With Abbott and I no longer around, John began to follow Andy's regiment. They even added in watching a sporting event or two in the casino's sports book, betting a little money so as to make the game more interesting. Both seemed to enjoy the company.

"If you sit here long enough," Andy said

while they sat next to the fountain in front of Caesar's Palace, "you can see half the world walk by. Everyone comes to Vegas sooner or later."

"I don't know about that. My parents never did," John said.

Andy laughed, "They must be in the other half." Something seemed on his mind. "So I've known you a week now, and I still have no idea what you do for a living."

"You're witnessing it."

"Talking to old men and people watching? Can't be much money in that," he chuckled.

"You'd be surprised. And I don't just limit myself to old men. Sometimes I talk to old women, and get them to be my sugar mama."

"Are you serious??"

"No, I'm not serious," John said, before adding after a slight pause for dramatic effect, "I'm a professional gambler."

It was the first time he had said it out loud, and he liked the way it sounded. It made him feel like a gunslinger in the old west.

"Well, you're certainly pretty good at it. You must be up 20 grand just in the time I've been with you."

"You do all right yourself."

"Yeah, I'm up about thirty-two bucks."

"That's what happens when you bet like an old man."

"I can't count cards," Andy said with a smile. "I can barely count to ten."

"What makes you think I can?"

"Well, it's either that, or you're the luckiest sonuvabitch I ever met."

"I am getting kind of tired of counting cards. My head is starting to ache. You ever play any poker? I hear that's the real man's game out here."

"I used to be in a weekly game and I watch it every week on ESPN," Andy answered.

"There's a qualifier for the Main Event of the World Series of Poker starting in an hour over at Harrah's. $300 buy-in. You interested?"

"Of course I'm interested," he grinned.

The qualifier drew 200 players, none of whom, with the exception of John, had the $10,000 entry fee it would take to enter the $10,000,000 Main Event that began the following Monday. At $300 a pop that meant the top six would qualify.

Three and a half hours into the tournament, 27 players remained, including both John and Andy. John glanced over at Andy's table and saw that Andy had a rather sizeable chip stack.

"The second hand of the tournament, I woke up with pocket Aces on the same hand that two other guys pushed All-In with pocket Kings," Andy explained during a break. "Can you believe it? They were both basically drawing dead before the flop. I haven't played a hand since."

John had a decent sized stack himself, but had amassed it with a more steady assault on his competition. If Andy was considered a "tight" player, the name given to someone who played very few hands, John was what was referred to as a "fish". He believed it was far better to bet on your hand after having seen five of the cards, rather than just two. As long as the blinds were small and there wasn't a huge raise, he would pay to see the flop. He was also difficult to play against, because he was unpredictable. Sometimes he would raise with a crap hand, and sometimes he would limp in with something good. Other times, he would do the opposite. His latest demolition of a player came when the player limped in with Ace/King suited and John called with pocket 8's, or "snowmen". When the flop came Ace, Ace, 8, giving John a Full House, he knew that unless the fourth Ace dropped or the board paired, the guy was going home. When neither happened, the guy stood up, shook his hand, and headed for the exit, thinking he had no one to blame but himself for limping in with a good hand. But the reality of it was that John might have called no matter what he had done.

An hour later, Andy and John both found themselves at the final table. Nine players remained. Six would win. Two players were short-stacked, and were soon eliminated. They needed to outlast one more player, but Andy was now the short-stack, having gotten whittled down by the increasing blinds. He soon found himself pot committed and All-In with John and one other person still in the hand. John's read was that Andy had a mediocre hand, but had to take a stand while he still had some chips left, hoping no one would call. When the other guy did call, John decided to jump in to save his friend. John had more than twice the chip stack of the other player, and he knew that unless the guy had a premium hand, there was no way he would call an All-In push from John and risk being knocked out on the bubble. If the guy called and John lost the hand, he would still make the final six, although Andy would be eliminated. But Andy was about to get eliminated anyway. John was his only hope.

"All-In," John said, calmly shoving all of his chips into the center of the table.

The man looked at him, and then seemed to be considering the possibilities for the briefest of moments before he folded. When Andy turned over pocket 7's, John breathed a sigh of relief. He only had 5's.

"What the hell were you thinking?!" the other guy scolded. "I had him beat."

"Then you should have called," John answered.

"You should have checked! What a stupid play," the man grumbled.

Technically, the man was right, but stupid plays were relative in poker. In this case, John's "stupid play" had helped earn both Andy and him seats in the Main Event. Poker wasn't meant to be a team sport, but what the hell.

XVIII
~THE RETURN OF NOSE HAIR~

Working the midnight shift at a radio station when you never were quite able to master sleeping during the afternoon was exhausting. Coaching 15 teenage girls for three months was a different kind of exhausting. But playing 10 hours of poker for four straight days with very few breaks was a combination of the two. His back ached. His vision was blurred. And he had a headache not caused by a blitzing lineman, but rather by trying to calculate pot odds and how many big blinds he had in his stack.

By the end of the 4th day, the field of 7,744 had been whittled to 774, which meant everyone left was going to get paid. John's initial $300 investment had already returned $14,996 and was going up with every person that was eliminated. He was effectively playing with house money now, as he pretty much had since he arrived a little more than a week ago.

"Do you ever lose at anything?" Andy asked him. Andy had made the money as well, but unlike John, who had galloped in, Andy more or less limped in like a horse that needed to be shot. Unless he could double up soon, Andy's tournament run would be over.

"Only in the game of life," John answered.

"I find that hard to believe."

"Believe it." John had two great fears in life. One was to succeed, because he hated the attention that went with it. The other was not succeeding, because he never wanted to find out that his best wasn't good enough. But until his recent run of success, he had rarely bothered to see if it was.

It was ironic that most people entered the World Series of Poker with dreams of a huge payday, but hopes of a small one. If somewhere along the way, they got to play a few hands against one of the pros and maybe get on ESPN, all the better. While John wasn't adverse to making money, it wasn't his driving force. His main objectives were actually in direct competition with each other. On one hand, he wanted to see how he would stack up against the top players in the world. On the other, was that he desperately didn't want the television exposure that would probably go along with succeeding against them.

"I tell you what," Andy said, "I've led a pretty good life. I married a woman I loved. I have two great kids. I ran a successful business. I got to travel the world—"

"You're not dying on me are you??" John asked.

"No, I'm not dying. But before I do, I'd like to smack Todd Mellman in a big hand of poker. I know he's the best, but the guy won't shut up. Bitches after every hand he loses as if people should just throw him their chips!" he said, flinging his arm into the air for dramatic effect. "And if possible, I'd like to do it on national television."

"Maybe you'll get to do exactly that."

"I don't have enough chips left to even put a dent in his stack."

"Hang around. Things can change in a hurry in this game."

Mellman was a former World Champion with a reputation for being good, but also a bit obnoxious. To some people, he was simply good and obnoxious. And John was partially right. Things did change for Andy, but it took two days for it to happen. By the time it did, they were down to the final two tables of players, 18 in all. At their table, in addition to the two of them, were two college kids who had qualified for the tournament online, two professional players, one of whom had won a World Series bracelet, a high school guidance counselor, a Hollywood talent agent, and in the irony of ironies; the man with the nose hair seated next to him on his flight into Vegas. Mellman was at the other table.

John had an average stack size when play started that Sunday afternoon. The blinds were huge. People were tired. And ESPN had begun to set up for their live coverage of the final table, while two cameras jumped between the two remaining tables. To that point, John had managed to mostly avoid being on TV simply by not being involved in any of the hands whenever the light on top of the camera turned red.

Seven hours later, only 11 people remained between the two tables. Six were at John and Andy's; the two pros, the agent, and Nose Hair.

"So, you're a Hollywood agent, eh?" John asked, during a hand they were both out of. "At which agency?"

"I'm at EAA," the man answered.

John didn't know much about Hollywood, but he knew EAA was the best.

"Tell me something, then. How do so many bad movies get made?"

"We don't smell 'em, we just sell 'em."

"Yeah, but after a few of them bomb, I would think they wouldn't want to smell what you're cookin."

"That's what I get paid to do. Sell them what they don't want to buy."

"It's just amazing to me. I can look at any trailer and tell you immediately whether the movie will make any money or not."

"The only problem with that is, by the time you see the trailer, the movie's already been made."

"I'm sure I could tell just from reading a script. In fact, I'll go one better than that. I could tell just from the tag line. Kid from the slums of India goes on *Who Wants to be a Millionaire* and wins because all of the questions end up being related to experiences from his life. Great idea. Low cost. Big hit. I would have snapped it up inside of five minutes if I was a studio head."

"How about The Wolfman?" the agent said, intrigued now.

"Too expensive. Not original. It's got Anthony Hopkins, but no one wants to see him in a trash movie like that. Bomb of epic proportions relative to its' cost."

"I've got one for you. A love story set on board the Titanic, between a rich girl and a boy from the streets."

"It'll never make it," John said, shaking his head sarcastically.

"You *are* good," the agent laughed.

The dealers had just dealt what was most likely going to be the last hand of the night. John glanced down at his two cards and saw what was considered to be the worst starting hand in Texas Hold 'Em Poker, the 2/7 off suit. He held the cards loosely as if they contained a fungus and prepared to toss them into the muck when the table suddenly came to life.

"Raise to six hundred thousand," the pro that was in the first seat said.

It was a raise six times the blinds.

"Call," said the agent.

"Call," said the second pro.

After Andy folded, Nose Hair called as well.

They had all called with such frightening speed, that only one thought went through John's mind. They were all chasing the same cards. John clutched his 2/7 a little more closely now, and decided to call.

The flop came out 5 of clubs, 2 of clubs, 7 of hearts and the pro in the first position immediately shoved All-In. The agent didn't hesitate to call. The second pro folded and Nose Hair called. John had more chips left than both Agent and Nose Hair, but less than the pro. What types of hands could they be playing, John wondered? He doubted any of them had played pocket sevens with that kind of raise. 2's and 5's were even less likely. He figured the pro had Aces or Kings. If anyone else had Aces, they would have pushed All-In pre-flop. Maybe one of the other two had Kings as well, in which case they were both drawing dead. And Nose Hair? Maybe Ace/King of clubs and he was now chasing a flush.

Any way he looked at it, John thought he was ahead going into the last two cards, and as long as the board didn't pair, he stood to win a boatload of chips, and unfortunately for him, a ton of face time on ESPN.

"I call," he said.

The 4th card was a 10 of diamonds. The final card was a 7 of clubs. The expression on all three of the others told John they each thought they might have won the hand.

"Turn them over," the dealer said.

The pro showed his pocket Aces. The agent mucked his hand, when he couldn't beat that. Nose Hair turned over an Ace and King of clubs for the nut flush and smiled—until John tossed his 2 and 7 onto the table for a Full House. The ballroom at Harrah's *erupted.*

"That's how you make a 2/7 pay," Andy remarked with a wink.

The pro did his best to disguise his disappointment, and immediately began replaying the hand in his head to see what he could have done differently. The agent stood up and shook John's hand.

"Nice hand. If you're ever in LA looking for a job in the movie industry, give me a call," he smiled.

"Will do."

John couldn't tell if Nose Hair was about to throw up or cry. After all, the difference between 9th place and 11th place was more than six hundred *thousand* dollars. That would teach him to look over John's shoulder while he was reading.

The Main Event was down to its final table and no matter what happened from there, both John and Andy were going to be very rich men.

XIX
~EVERY DONKEY HAS HIS DAY~

The knocking at the door was barely audible at first, but was growing louder with each successive knock. Whoever it was must have initially been worried about waking up the other people on the floor of the hotel since it was 5:00am, before they realized light knocking was not going to wake John.

He tried to rub the sleep from his eyes before looking through the peephole to see who was there. And unless his eyes were playing tricks on him, he couldn't believe who was on the other side of the door.

"Coach?" he said, as he opened it.

Jim Carson didn't wait to be invited in. "We lost again," he said.

"I saw. Out of curiosity, how did you find me?" John asked.

"ESPN, numbnuts."

"Weren't you coaching?"

"There's this invention called a DVR. And I never miss an episode of the World Series of Poker."

John nodded. He should have thought about that. But it was early, and he was tired. He wondered how many other people had seen it. Damn ESPN. The first time they ever decided to show the thing live. "So what can I do for you, coach?"

"As you are well aware, we only have one game left, and there's a lot on the line. We need to win to make the playoffs. If we do, Wally will get his contract renewed and we all stand to make considerable bonuses. But more importantly, it would give the city of Cleveland a chance to finally restore some of its lost pride. It's a proud city, John, filled with good people. They deserve this."

"Sure they do. But how can I help?"

"By playing," Carson said simply.

"What about Campbell?"

"Done. Blew out his knee again."

"And Adams?"

"When you first called me six months ago, never in a million years did I ever think I'd be saying this, but....Adams....isn't....you."

"Thanks, coach, and I really wish I could help, but—"

"I know you're not hurt," Carson said. "I could tell from the angle I had when you went down. But I figured you had your reasons, and I figured we should be able to win one game without you. But we haven't been able to. Now, I don't know what caused you to start playing football again after all these years. Maybe it was a publicity stunt..."

"I'm not going back to the radio station," John assured him.

"Well, maybe it was to impress some girl. Maybe it was part of some early mid-life crisis. Or maybe it was just to prove something to yourself. I don't know the reason, and quite frankly, I don't really care. What I do know is that we're playing the Baltimore Ravens on Sunday night. The same Baltimore Ravens who used to be the Cleveland Browns and left the city for greener pastures, taking with them a city's sense of identity and source of pride. We need to beat them. And I think our chances are better with you than without."

"What about Wally and the rest of the guys?"

"I'm sure some of them saw you on TV. And I'm sure they're plenty pissed. But I'm also sure that if you help them win Sunday, all will be forgiven."

"And if we lost?"

"They'd probably want to kill you, but I'm sure they already do anyway, so what do you have to lose?"

"I have to think about it, coach."

"What's to think about?"

"I have to be somewhere next week. I couldn't stay for the playoffs if we won."

"Why not?"

"I can't really explain right now, but someday soon, I'll tell you everything, I promise."

Carson thought it over for a few seconds.

"Listen, if you help us this week, I'll drive you to the airport myself after the game and get you on a flight wherever you want to go. No one cares about the playoffs this year. It's getting in that's important."

"I'm also at the final table of the World Series of Poker. Nine people are left. If I win, I'll make 10 *million* dollars."

"And if you come in 9th, you still make 900 thousand."

"Nine-hundred thousand will buy you a nice house. 10 million will buy you a nice life."

"So win quickly and get your ass to Cleveland."

"It doesn't really work that way," John said, knowing Carson was aware of that. "Besides, I haven't practiced in more than two weeks. You saw how rusty Campbell was."

"Campbell was coming off an injury. As we both know, you're not."

John was conflicted. He was worried he wouldn't play well if he went back, and he really didn't want to live on in infamy as The Goat of Cleveland. Plus, he knew he could help Andy at the final table if he stayed. Help a city or help a friend. Then again, coach was a friend too. Bottom line was he felt his old insecurity creeping back in. What if his best wasn't good enough?

"I don't know, coach," he finally said. "I'll try, but I think I'd plan to play without me."

Jim Carson nodded a disappointed nod as if

he had been punched in the gut by a close friend.
He didn't say another word as he let himself out.

*   *   *

"Are you kidding me?!" Mellman bellowed
as the kid from RPI shoved all in after the River
card. "You chased a straight all the way down to
the river??"

The kid smiled sheepishly. Everyone else
looked a bit uncomfortable.

"Ok, kid. You can have this pot. And please
keep playing that way. Next time when you miss,
I'll gladly take all your chips."

"Please give me just one hand against him
with enough chips to do some damage," Andy
mumbled under his breath, just loudly enough
for the people on his side of the table to hear.

"You say something, Andy?" Mellman asked
accusingly.

"Just nice lay down, Todd," Andy answered,
winking at John with the eye that faced away from
the former World Champion.

There was no questioning Mellman's talent.
He had the ability to read people like no one
John had ever played against. Granted, most of
the people John had played against before the
past week were bar flies and beach bums who
thought a "straight" was a way you took your
drink. But he was such an a-hole, trying to
intimidate everyone he played. Maybe that was
part of the reason for his success. Embarrassing
people into playing the way he wanted them to

play. Knowing that certainly didn't make playing against him any more enjoyable.

Things weren't exactly moving along at a blistering pace. Eight players still remained, after an accountant from Duluth, Minnesota took a bow and headed home with $921,343. Of the eight, John and Andy were in 4th and 3th place respectively. John had been playing a little more carelessly than usual and had lost a fair number of chips because of it. Andy was his usual tight self, playing very few hands, which was why everyone took notice when he suddenly shoved all of his chips into the middle.

"I'm all-in," he said.

Andy was a tough read for most people. Not much flustered him after Korea and Vietnam, and he certainly wasn't going to worry about a hand in a game of poker. While others shook and trembled when making a move, Andy could have performed surgery. His hands and face belied nothing.

And his reputation for playing tightly throughout the tournament--meaning he usually played only premium hands--was a reason to respect him whenever he did play a hand. Everyone folded around to John, who was smiling.

There were few things in life John was sure about these days, but he knew one thing for certain. Andy had rockets. There was no way he would risk his tournament life on anything less, and he wasn't about to limp in with them. It was how he lived his life. John took one last glance at his 7 of hearts and 4 of spades.

"I call," he said, still smiling.

"Turn them over," the dealer told them.

You could hear the collective gasp in the room when John showed his cards. Even Andy was confused as he turned over two Aces. The Aces held up, Andy was now the chip leader, and John was eliminated in 8th place. All told, his $300 investment would pay him more than 1.1 million dollars.

Andy stood to shake his friend's hand and John pulled him in for hug. "Play well with my chips," he whispered.

"I don't understand," Andy answered. "Why?"

"I just realized I have somewhere I need to be." And he added, "And you need to take down Mellman."

"Where are you going?"

"Make sure you watch the Browns game tonight, and maybe throw a couple of grand on them if you're feeling lucky," was John's response.

"What does that have to do with anything??" Andy asked.

"Can we get back to poker now?" Mellman interrupted.

"Just watch the game and you'll understand," John repeated.

Andy watched as his friend made his way past

the scattered applause of the crowd and ESPN's announcers, who were undoubtedly killing him for what might have gone down as the worst call in the history of poker. Andy was suddenly blinded by the flash of a camera, and by the time he regained his vision, his friend had disappeared into the deep shadows of the room.

*   *   *

If John had walked into a high school locker room after leaving the team for two weeks, half the team would have wanted to fight him; the other half would have asked him to leave. Pro football players asked only two things. Don't fumble. And score touchdowns. While a few of them still played because they loved the game, most of them saw it as a way to make as much money as possible in the time they had. And if they thought someone could help them make more of it, they would have welcomed Mussolini himself into the backfield.

The story went that John really *did* have a concussion and went home to rest. While he was there, he ran into an old friend who decided to run off to Vegas with his fiancée to get married and asked him to come along as the best man. Once in Vegas, he played in a poker tournament and ended up qualifying for the Main Event, which happened to be out there at the same time. The rest, they saw on ESPN. It was a bit far fetched, but John had learned early in life when lying, throw in as much useless detail as possible. Most people weren't creative enough to do that, so they figured no one else was either. It helped that Jimbo, one of the leaders on the team, not to mention the largest, welcomed him back.

"Welcome back, poker star," he said.

It also didn't hurt that a national audience had seen him toss away a chance at winning nine million dollars just so he could come back and play with the Browns. Not many of them would have done the same.

The game itself was a foregone conclusion that night. John knew it as soon as he jogged onto the field to a standing ovation. The Greatest Mann in the World had returned and an entire city was metaphorically standing on the sideline behind him. When John scored a touchdown in the first quarter, the Ravens knew it as well.

Up ten points in the fourth quarter, John took a handoff and cut inside Jimbo's block. He darted for five yards, but as he was going down, a linebacker and two linemen landed on him with his leg in an awkward position. John heard the crack in his ankle that X-Rays would later confirm was broken, but stayed in the game anyway.

"Just tape it as tight as you can," he told the trainer.

When it was over, the Browns were in the playoffs, a city celebrated, and John was in a walking cast headed to the airport. He turned on ESPN while he waited in the lounge for his flight to board.

"The Browns, yes, you heard me correctly, the Browns, those of Cleveland, are headed to the playoffs," Chris Berman announced. "John 'The Greatest Mann in the World' scored a touchdown in his return from the poker room. More on that and all the other scores from week 17 on Sports Center in 30 minutes. But now, we return to the World Series of Poker's Main Event...."

Two players remained. Andy, who had only played two hands since he had eliminated John, and Todd Mellman. Todd had done the dirty work, eliminating the other five players himself, while Andy stood pat. Thanks to John, he still had about a thousand more chips than Mellman.

The next hand was dealt. The camera beneath the table showed Mellman had pocket 7's. Andy decided to look at his cards out of the camera's view, so no one could see what he had.

"Raise to two million," Mellman said.

"Call," Andy answered.

"I have no idea what he has!" ESPN's announcer screamed.

The flop was 4 of diamonds, 5 of hearts and 7 of clubs.

"I'll go to 5 mill," Mellman said, with the glint in his eye of someone who now had three 7's.

"What the heck, Toddy. I'll go all-In," Andy responded with very little hesitation.

The room at Harrah's Casino went wild. The 20 or so people in the airport lounge in Cleveland did as well.

"Oh, Andy," Mellman groused, "I really hope for your sake you don't have Aces again. Because this time, they won't be good enough. I call."

Everything seemed to move in slow motion at that instant. The dealer turning and burning the remaining cards—a 10 of hearts and a 2 of spades. Mellman slapping his two 7's down on the table for trips. Andy dropping his 3 of hearts and 6 of diamonds onto the table in front of the dealer.

Most of the audience didn't even see it at first. But Mellman did. So did John 2,500 miles away. 3...4...5...6...7. Andy had a straight.

"Are you fucking kidding me??!!!" Mellman screamed, as ESPN censors dove for the mute button. "You called that raise with a 3/6 offsuit??? You mother _ _ _ _ _ _ !"

The rest of the audio sounded like Moby concert. Beep. Beep. Beep. Beeeeeeep. John almost fell out of his chair he was laughing so hard.

"Now boarding, flight 1722 to Los Angeles through Gate 5," the loudspeaker bellowed.

"Atta boy, Andy," John said to no one in particular, as he exited the lounge and headed for his plane.

XX
~CASHING IN HIS CHIPS~

Jerry Weinberg was a Harvard law grad who was named to Hollywood's Power List for the first time when he was only 28 years old. By the time he was 40, he was a full partner at Entertainers and Athletes Agency—Hollywood's largest and most powerful talent agency. His client roster was a veritable who's who of A list producers, directors, actors, actresses and writers, and he himself was linked to an Oscar winning actress. His appointment schedule was booked for weeks in advance, but he made time when he got the call from his former tablemate at the World Series of Poker. He agreed to meet John for lunch.

"I have to admit, when I told you to call me the next time you were in town, I didn't think it was going to be three days later," he said as John limped up to his table in a walking cast.

"I figured I'd strike while the iron was hot," John said.

"What'd you do to your ankle?" Jerry asked, motioning towards John's cast. "Kick the table after you got eliminated?"

"Tripped over my dog going down the stairs."

"Ouch. So tell me why you want to be an agent?"

"Because I can't dance."

"And what do you know about the industry?"

"I know that the studios are backing away from big budget movies, because with advertising, they have to make back double the cost of the movie just to break even. Hence the glut of Rom-Coms. I also know that *Avatar* has made more money than any movie in history, but that *Gone With the Wind* has sold more tickets because it has been re-released four times."

"I read *Daily Variety* too," Jerry said. "Now tell me something the average person in the industry wouldn't know."

"They wouldn't know that every good project is driven by a good script. The streets of Hollywood are littered with movie flops that had A list talent and a poor script. But rarely is the reverse true, with the notable exception being *The Last Boy Scout.*"

"You read that script?" he asked, intrigued now.

"A friend of mine who used to work at UTA sent it to me. It was a great script. They just did a lousy job making it."

"Anything else?"

"Just that sales is all about relationships. And it doesn't matter if you're selling tires, heating oil, office furniture or movies. The one gift I've always had is that I can put my finger on the pulse of the idiots in society. Of course, my dad might have argued that's because I'm one of them, but still..."

"If true, that would be a tremendous asset," Jerry laughed. "The idiots of society make up about 95% of our audience. Now you want to hear what I know about you?"

"I'm not sure," John cringed. "Do I?"

"I know that you're the only person in Connecticut history to have won a high school basketball state championship as both a coach and player. I know that you went to Yale and were a two-time All-American football player there. I know that you had a syndicated radio show in Dallas. I know that you're a pretty good poker player when you want to be. And I know that you broke your ankle leading the Cleveland Browns to victory last night."

John wasn't quite sure how to respond, so he chose not to say anything.

"What I don't know is why you're here."

"My season's over, and so is my football career."

"A career that lasted 16 games, only eight of which you played in. And just like that, it's over?"

"I'm 33 years old. I'll be 34 before next season."

"Some guys play into their late 30's."

"I don't want to be one of those guys who walks with a limp the rest of his life," John explained.

"Then why play at all? Was it some sort of

bet?"

"What are you, a reporter?"

"It's all public information. Most people just don't bother to check. But we aren't selling $120 tires here. We're selling $50 million movies. So, what about all the other stops? No offense, John, but you seem like kind of a flake."

"Just some things I always wanted to try. Turns out, they weren't what I thought they'd be—except for maybe one of them. But I'm home now."

Jerry seemed to be mulling it over in his mind. He had always prided himself on being an excellent read of people. It was one of the things that made him a good poker player. "Turns out you're in luck," he said at last. "One of our Junior Agents left yesterday to become a partner at The Gersh Agency. So I have an opening in my department. It's in Packaging. You know what that is?"

John had read about it. EAA was famous for it. "Putting together entire projects; Script, Producers, Director, Actors and pitching the entire thing to a studio."

"Exactly. And there aren't many more difficult things to do in the industry than trying to sell a studio head on an actress when they have someone else in mind for the role. But the more people in the project we have attached that are represented by us, the more money we make as an agency."

"I understand."

"You think you could do that?"

"I could sell a catsup popsicle to an Eskimo in a white tuxedo."

"Something tells me you probably could," Jerry laughed. "Besides, you're a hot ticket now. Might be able to parlay this into some publicity for the agency. May be a movie in it." He motioned with his head. "Follow me."

"Here's your office," Jerry said, sweeping his arm across the desk and dumping all sorts of scripts, paper, pens and pictures onto the floor. "Janice! Get somebody in here to pack up Josh's crap and leave it in a box out by the elevators. Ungrateful little prick that he was."

It was a pretty nice office, as far as offices went. Beautifully furnished. Well-lit. With a great view of the Hollywood Hills.

"Let me show you something," Jerry said.

John followed him to a storage closet down the hall.

Inside were scripts by the hundreds.

"You said a script is the most important part of a project. Inside this closet is every unsolicited script and their tag line, that we've received in the past two weeks. Go find a winner."

Prisoners race cars to determine who is paroled and who is killed to solve overcrowding in the prison system. Think The Running Man meets Days of Thunder.

Good God, John thought.

The female hairstylist to the ultra conserva-

tive President of the United States has an affair with the First Lady.

Not sure how broad the appeal would be for that one.

American soldiers capture the new head of Al Queda and bring him to New York City where citizens pay $50 each for the right to beat him.

Although he agreed with the concept, he might have a difficult time selling that one to liberals who were against capital punishment and torture.

A disgraced fighter pilot who is dishonorably discharged from the Air Force for flying too dangerously, becomes the head of the New York City cabby union.

What?

And then finally...

A high school teacher dies while saving the life of a little boy and is rewarded by being given the opportunity to go back and re-live any five days of his life.

Thought provoking. It had promise. He sat down on a pile of scripts and read the first ten pages. Then he read ten more. After sitting in the closet for an hour and a half, he was sold.

He walked into Jerry's office and held up the script. "I've got a winner," he announced.

"Pete. Let me call you back," Jerry said to the person he was talking to. And then to John, "Just like that, huh?"

"When you know, you know."

"Pitch it to me."

"It's the story of a high school teacher who dies while saving a little boy from drowning, and is rewarded by being given the opportunity to re-live any five days of his life."

"I'm still listening," Jerry said, and John could almost see the wheels spinning in his head.

"The days he chooses are days from recent history that most of us would remember. 9/11. The day the US Hockey team beat the Russians in the Olympics. The day of *The Police's* sold out concert at Shea Stadium when they were the biggest rock band in the world. We get to see why those days were important to him, and also remind us where we were on those days. It's got romance, drama, sharp dialogue....everything."

"That's nice, but why should we make it? Any studio exec is going to want to know."

"Because it will have a broad appeal to both men and women. Women for the romance, and men, because what man wouldn't like a do-over in life?"

"That it?"

"We could get a great cast who would probably be willing to cut their rates to take back-end points. It wouldn't cost much to make, leaving the possibility of making a ton of money."

"Now you're talking their language. Who do you see in the leads?"

"Ben Affleck, Luke Wilson, or Matt Dillon for the male lead."

"Affleck is repped by WME. Wilson or Dillon could work. What about the female lead?"

"Only one comes to mind. Joely Beckett."

"Nice try."

"She's repped here isn't she?"

"Not for long. Think of someone else."

"I'm telling you, she's the one."

"That will be a tough sell to any studio. JoBe has a worse reputation than LiLo."

"Not only will I get her, but I'll get her to do it for free."

"I don't know what you're smoking, but I'd love to have some," Jerry laughed.

"Get us in the door at one of the studios and I'll sell it."

That was one thing Jerry could do. It didn't matter who they were talking to; studio executives jumped off any call when Jerry Weinberg was on the other line.

"Leave the script," Jerry said. He glanced at the cover. "*An Ordinary Life*? We need to change the title."

"I like it," John told him. "It's a play on the fact that what the guy had always considered to be an ordinary life, turned out to be anything but, when he could only choose five days from it."

"And what five days would you pick? Any regrets in your life?" Jerry asked.

"Too many for just five days, I'll tell you that much."

"Well, you could always go looking for a

drowning boy to save," Jerry winked.

XXI
˜THE BOYS OF SUMNER˜

On the streets of 1960's Brooklyn, Sumner Stein quickly learned that if you weren't the toughest kid on the block, you better make sure everyone thought you were. It was there that he learned to talk a pretty good game.

"You don't know me. I'll kill you!" was a favorite phrase of his.

His thinking was that people always feared the unknown. If they didn't know what he was capable of, most people wouldn't wait to find out.

But once Vinnie Fiorillo called him out on his threat and beat him senseless in 9th grade, Sumner's father gave him some advice.

"Always make friends with the biggest guy in the room, because you never know when you'll need him." He also added, "And don't gamble against a rich man, because he won't care if he loses."

Both were sound pieces of advice that he never forgot. The first one helped him survive high school, while the second helped him eventually build the empire that would come to be known as Sunshine Valley Pictures.

He learned in 2nd grade when he was the last one chosen in dodgeball that he would never be a professional athlete. And he learned he would never be an artist in the 6th grade when his stick figure renditions weren't very well received. But even though, or maybe because, he wasn't artistically inclined, he always admired those who were. After graduation from the Wharton School of Business, he went directly to Beverly Hills and took a job in the mailroom at the William Morris Agency.

Talent agencies were the last businesses that truly operated on the caste system. The mailroom was the first tier, and it paid lawyers, MBA's, former stockbrokers, and graduates of Harvard, Yale, Notre Dame and Stanford minimum wage. Responsibilities included the obvious; such as delivering mail, to the less obvious; such as delivering oversized pink teddy bears to a studio head's daughter for her 3rd birthday. The second tier was called, "getting on a desk"—otherwise known as becoming a Junior Agent. It paid slightly more than minimum wage for 12 hour days in which you answered 200 phone calls, scheduled 100 appointments for your boss, typed 25 contracts, and lied to everyone else about everything in order to make your boss look organized and better than he actually was.

The one perk to being on a desk, was that it was the first time you were actually asked to read scripts for clients. You'd see them coming through the mailroom, and could glance at them on a break, but no one ever asked what you thought about them. While on a desk, the senior agents asked you to read 20 of them each weekend, then asked your opinion of them the following Monday, although they largely ignored said opinion. They had predetermined what script was best for their client based on who was directing and producing it. They just needed summaries of the other ones, so they would have justification for rejecting them. It was this very system that spawned the phrase, "We don't smell 'em, we just sell 'em." It was also this phrase that caused five junior agents to take information on 50 unheralded clients and leave under the cover of night to form their own rival agency.

The partners at their old agency initially scoffed at the mutiny. The clients that went with the junior agents weren't important to them anyway. But Sumner and the others in the "EAA 5" as they were dubbed, saw something in each of these clients that they knew they could develop. And develop they did, to the tune of $100 million dollars a year by their 5th year in business, doubling what the old place brought in annually. It was then, that Sumner decided to strike out on his own once again. He was tired of trying to sell people's work. He wanted to be the one buying it, and armed with the support of the EAA client roster, he accepted a job as the Vice President of Development for the then little known Sunshine Valley Pictures.

His first film was a $40,000 independent film from a student at NYU film school, starring a soon-to-be megastar male lead. The film went on to gross $25 million, which was a nifty return on the initial investment. When his second film was a Scorsese directed thriller that garnered three academy award nominations along with $300 million dollars worldwide, his ascension to the top of the Hollywood ladder was complete. Of course with success, came the pressure to remain successful. For every costly flop, he needed five hits. It was an average that would have made him the best hitter in the Baseball Hall of Fame by more than 200 percentage points. It was also probably the reason he hated weathermen so much. They had nowhere near that success rate, and yet, always managed to keep their jobs.

Sumner snapped open his copy of *Daily Variety* and relaxed at his desk. Steam rose from the fresh cup of coffee in front of him.

"Mr. Stein," the intercom buzzed, "Jerry Weinberg and John Mann are here."

Sumner leaned forward. "Send them in," he answered, folding the trade magazine in half before placing it down in front of him.

"Gentlemen," he said as he rose to greet them.

"How are you, Sumner?" Jerry asked.

"I'm ok for someone who's lost 200 million in the stock market."

"So that only leaves you with 800 million," Jerry smirked.

"You can never have too much money, Jerry. Have a seat. So, I read the script you sent over."

"And?" Jerry asked.

"And it's good. I like the premise."

Jerry motioned to John to take the reins.

"Think *It's a Wonderful Life* meets *Forest Gump*," John offered.

"Those are some pretty hefty films to compare it to," Sumner said.

"We think it's that good."

Sumner wasn't convinced. "Who's the lead?" he asked.

"Luke Wilson has just signed on," Jerry said.

"How's he going to find time to make a movie with all those AT&T commercials he's filming?" Sumner snarked. He didn't seem all that impressed. "And the female lead?"

"Joely Beckett," John told him.

"JoBe? What makes you think she'll do it? I heard she's been turning down everything that comes her way. She's got a great presence, but she's becoming a train wreck."

"She'll make our movie. We're meeting her at the Ivy in 40 minutes."

"You seem pretty sure of that."

"I'm as sure as sunshine," John answered.

"What are the asking prices?"

"Five mill for Wilson and nothing for Beckett."

"You think she's going to do your project out

"of the goodness of her heart?" Sumner asked incredulously.

"Just make a nice donation to her favorite charity instead," John said.

Even Jerry didn't seem convinced of that.

"That doesn't sound like her. Does she know that?"

"She will in about 40 minutes."

"I don't even want to know. And only five million for Wilson?"

"He wants back end points."

"I'm sure he does. Find me someone who doesn't."

"He's perfect for the role," John responded. "Besides, I would think you would want someone who believes in the project enough that he's willing to take less up front."

"Where'd you find this guy, Jerry?" Sumner laughed. "If the movie's really a money-maker like you told me on the phone, then I want all the profits. I certainly don't want to be sharing them with some commercial actor."

"Then you'll have to pay him more up front," John said. They were trying to find the balance between working for their client and getting the project made.

"I don't *have* to pay him anything."

"You don't want to be the guy who passed on this," Jerry interjected. "Especially since we've come to you first."

There were two undeniable truths in Hollywood. The first, was that no one wanted to go out of their way to help anyone. The second, was that no one wanted to be the one who passed on the next big project.

"It shouldn't be just about money, should it?" John asked.

"Not just about money? Of course it is. Everything is about money." Sumner truly believed that.

"Shouldn't it be about quality too?"

"Quality is over-rated," Sumner said as he poured himself a drink. "Anyone want anything?"

"A little early in the morning for me, Sumner," Jerry said.

There was a long silence while Sumner sipped his Dewar's on the rocks. By the time he turned around to face them they knew they had a deal. "You sign Joely Beckett for the terms we spoke of and we'll make the movie."

The Ivy was one of the three or four places the Hollywood elite went to broker movie deals. Meeting for a drink happened at all hours of the day. Lunch was for the real power brokers. Getting a table was a near impossibility unless you were an *A Lister* or a tabloid regular. Joely Beckett fell into the latter category, her partying prowess far out shadowing her acting ability.

She was 22, blond and beautiful, with eyes that were a brilliant shade of crystal clear blue that had the ability to freeze your thought process mid sentence. Unfortunately, she also had a personality that screamed lobotomy.

"We're meeting Joely Beckett," Jerry said to the hostess.

She ushered them right in.

"She's waiting for you," she said, giving John the once over look of someone who couldn't quite place where she knew him from.

With a pastel, flowing sundress and an Annette Funicello style headband from the 60's, she could have been the girl next door—until she opened her mouth.

"Thanks for coming down," Jerry said as he offered his hand.

She shook it loosely, merely glancing at John over the top of her sunglasses.

"I was in the area," she answered bluntly. "So what's this project?"

"It's the story of a high school teacher who dies while saving a little boy from drowning, and is rewarded by being given the opportunity to re-live any five days of his life."

"That doesn't sound like much of a project for a female," she said.

"Actually, the female lead is a scene stealer. It's a great role."

"And who's the male lead?" she asked.

"Luke Wilson," Jerry answered.

"Luke Wilson??" she said.

"He's a good actor."

"You mean, he's with EAA and you want to keep it all in the family."

"He's perfect for the role," John added.

"Who *are* you?" she asked sharply.

"I'm John Mann. Nice to meet you," he said.

She ignored his response as if he hadn't said a word. She was probably the only person in America who *didn't* know who he was at that very moment.

"What's the salary?" she asked.

"Well, here's the thing," John said. "Nothing."

"Let me get this straight. You want to pay me nothing to make a movie with some B-lister male lead?" she asked, exasperated. "Am I on Punk'd? Where's Ashton?"

"We thought it would be a good thing if you donated your salary to a charitable cause."

"Oh you did, did you? Well, maybe I should start looking for different representation then. Thanks for wasting my time," she said as she got up to leave.

"Listen, you're a beautiful actress who has great screen presence. But from what I hear, you're headed down a coke laden path of self destruction that will either result in you pissing your career away, or dying before you turn 30 if you're not careful," John said as Jerry nearly choked.

"I appreciate your concern. Really, I do. *Not.*"

"I'm going to be very blunt with you," John began.

"Yes, you were so subtle before," Joely

answered.

"You've been arrested for DUI twice in the last three months. The second time resulted in serious injuries for the driver of the other car. You're headed to jail, Joely. But if you do this movie and donate your salary, we might be able to keep you out."

"Might? That's the best you can do?" she said.

"It's the best offer you're going to get. And the offer is good for the next ten seconds only," John said, thrusting a contract across the table for her to sign.

She didn't say a word. Jerry himself looked both uncomfortable and impressed at the same time.

As if to make a very small point, she signed the paper after *eleven* seconds had passed.

XXII
˜THE PRODIGAL SON
RETURNS˜

Two weeks later, the deal was announced in *Daily Variety*. That night, John returned to *The Shanty* for the first time in nearly a year and a half. It was a turn away crowd, as Abbott and I poured drinks by the dozens. People were celebrating as if the Lakers had just won the World Championship again. John entered the bar to a standing ovation that rivaled any he had ever received. As the crowd cleared a path to the bar itself, John noticed an old friend.

"Is that your Bentley out back?" John asked.

Andy laughed. "In Los Angeles, it's more important to have a nice car than a nice house, because you spend more time in your car."

"What idiot told you that?"

"The same idiot who would call an All-In raise with a 7/4 offsuit at the final table of the World Series of Poker's Main Event."

"Which brings me to my next question," John said. "What on earth possessed you, the tightest of the tight players, to call Mellman's raise with a 3/6?"

"This guy I know is always talking about how much better it is to bet after seeing five cards instead of just two."

"Now what idiot said *that*?"

Andy smiled. "The same idiot."

"So how nice was it to crack Mellman?"

"You have no idea."

The two men hugged. Not a man hug, but a full-fledged hug between two people who were kindred spirits, showing that age was merely a number.

"How come you didn't tell me you played for the Browns?" Andy asked.

"Don't you ever watch ESPN?"

"It's Cleveland. I bet there isn't a person in this bar who could name three players on the Browns. Besides, I'm a Chargers fan."

"Well, there's probably a few other things you don't know about my employment history," John said, less than enthusiastically. He wasn't as proud of it as he thought he would be, because of how it affected other people.

"I heard all about it from your friends," Andy said. "What was it like? Did you ever wake up confused as to where you were and what you were doing?"

"All the time," John lamented. "And they were all great in their own way. Being a pro athlete was a trip. Thousands of people cheering and jeering your every move. Signing autographs. Having women throw themselves at you. Getting paid to play a game."

"There doesn't sound like too much of a downside to that," Andy laughed.

"Only the lack of privacy. That and I think if you experience it long enough, it's probably difficult to live without once your playing days are done."

"I could see that. What about the other jobs?"

"Being a DJ was cool. It was fun to bullshit with people. To say whatever popped into my head. To play music and joke and laugh. No real downside to it except working the midnight shift sucks."

"Out of all of them, which did you like the best?"

"I'd have to say working at the high school. I just felt like I actually made a difference there."

"And the girl?"

"What girl?"

"*The* girl. The one you couldn't stop talking about."

"She'll never speak to me again," John said.

"You don't know that."

"Yes, I do. I just left. For some juvenile bet."

"Listen. When I was in high school many, many, many years ago, this girl asked me to our Spring Fling. I told her I couldn't go because I was going to be visiting relatives that weekend. The truth of the matter was that I wanted to go get drunk with my buddies."

"Did you guys drink Moonshine back then?"

John asked with a sarcastic wink.

"I didn't grow up in the Old West. We drank Vodka. Anyway, when we were good and drunk, we thought it would be a good idea to crash the dance. And when that girl saw me, if she could have killed me with her eyes, she would have. But I apologized, and eventually, she forgave me. That girl, eventually became my wife. The point being, women have an amazing capacity to forgive where men are concerned, because they know even old men are little boys at heart. And little boys do stupid things."

It was at that moment, that Abbott climbed onto the bar in order to get everyone's attention.

"Its great to see you all again," he screamed over the noise that gradually quieted. "You know when we first set this bet up a little more than a year ago, I thought to myself; *'There is no way in hell, he's going to be able to pull this off.'* At least I sure hoped he couldn't," he added to laughter. "I'll admit it. I bet against him. Because as the men in this room can attest, there's nothing like winning a bet against your buddy, whether it's for pride, a dollar, a grand, or a million bucks."

John smiled sheepishly.

"But as it went on, I saw him do so many incredible things. Some in person. Who'd have thought John would have the patience to coach teenage girls? Date them maybe, but coach them? Not a chance. But he did it. And he won. And he somehow got his own radio show in Dallas. And he was successful at that. He didn't even tell us, but Nick and I figured it out when we heard his show syndicated in *Los Angeles.* The NFL? Are you serious? Unbelievable is all I can say. If I hadn't seen it with my own eyes, I would never have believed it. Making the final table at the World Series of Poker? Of course he did piss it all away at the end, but at least he did so to a good guy and for a good cause. John also made the people of Cleveland forget who LeBron James ever was. At any rate, he may not be a Governor, but he probably could be. Ladies and gentlemen, here he is—The Chameleon—John Mann!"

John leapt onto the bar top next to Abbott and the room fell silent again the way it always did whenever someone did something you admired.

"I had no idea what to expect when I first agreed to this silly bet fourteen months ago," John began. "And make no mistake about it. It was silly. But I guess there were two driving forces behind it. One was that you can't back down on a challenge from your friends," he said to laughter. "The other, was that I think all of us at one time or another, has wondered if we were capable of doing more with our lives. And then a funny thing happened along the way. In addition to meeting many incredible people from all walks of life, I came to the realization that sometimes less is more. And here's what I mean by that. You don't need to be Governor or

President to make a difference. You just need to like what you do, and do it the best you can. It doesn't matter if you collect trash, build roofs, or sell paper towel dispensers. What does matter, is that you do it well. That's how you make a difference."

John noticed that he was losing the attention of the crowd. They didn't want a lecture. They wanted to celebrate someone doing things most of them had only dreamed about doing.

"But tonight isn't about reflection," he continued, "It's about celebrating. And on that note, I've instructed Nick to return everyone's money from the bet. Your money is no good here. FOOD and DRINKS...are on the house!" he said to a thunderous roar.

*　　*　　*

Eighteen months later, *Five Days*, as it was now called, premiered in Los Angeles three days before Christmas. It was attended by a who's who of celebrities from Hollywood's *A list* to professional athletes and reality television stars. It was strictly black tie. Fifteen minutes before the movie previews began, the theatre was full, save for a row of reserved seats in the middle of the room for the film's producer, director, actors, and of course a high school coach, a radio DJ, a pro football player, a professional gambler and a Hollywood agent. The last five people needed only one seat.

XXIII
˜THE CHAMELEON˜

Time Magazine put John on the cover as soon as word of his exploits got out. It didn't take long. They had five pictures of him checkerboard style, each depicting him at one of his jobs. Wearing a shirt and tie while coaching. A t-shirt and jeans in front of a radio microphone. Shaking off a would be tackler for the Browns. A half-zip fleece with sunglasses and a baseball cap pulled down low at the poker table. And an Armani suit standing in front of Mann's Chinese Theatre (no relation).

At least ten other magazines did feature stories on him. He rapidly had become the most well-known celebrity in the country. His "fifteen minutes of fame" was set to last much longer. Job offers poured in from all over. But John had other plans.

His cell phone rang. He glanced down and saw the word "Hubbard" flash across the screen. John figured there was no time like the present for an explanation.

"Hubbard, my man!" he said.

"Don't Hubbard my man, me, you crazy bastard! So I'm at the newsstand this morning checking out Miss January, when whose ugly mug do I see staring back at me from the cover of *Time Magazine?*"

"I know. I know. And I apologize. If I could have explained, I would have."

"It would have been easier to track you down on *The Amazing Race.* Hermosa Beach. Salisbury. Dallas. Cleveland. Still don't know what you were thinking with that one. Couldn't you have hooked on with the Cowboys? Vegas. Hollywood. Jesus H. Where are you now?"

"I'm back in Hermosa Beach."

"Well, get your ass on a plane and get to Connecticut next Wednesday. Your friend the Governor is honoring my State Championship baseball team and OUR State Championship basketball team at a luncheon."

"I read that you won the state title. That's awesome. Congrats!"

"It was no minor accomplishment, believe you me, trying to coach while doing your job too."

"My job?"

"That goofy bastard Kovac has me doing it."

"Why hasn't he hired someone?"

"You know him. If he thought he could save thirty grand, he'd make his mother drive a wheelchair to work. And maybe there's a part of him that for some reason, still thinks you're coming back."

"How is Kovac?"

"Just as big a pain in the ass as ever."

"How's everyone else?"

"Why don't you just come out and ask how Melissa is?"

"How is she?"

"She's fine."

"Is she dating anyone?"

"Nope. And it's not like she hasn't had suitors. But don't worry, I've managed to chase them all off for you. Told one of them she had a scorching case of Herpes."

"What do you mean for me?" John asked.

"Listen, you goofy bastard," Hubbard said, "You're a nice enough guy and all, but do you really think I've been calling you five times a day for the past month because I missed you?"

"Then why have you been calling?"

"Because I'm tired of doing your job, and I'm tired of chasing off all these guys from your girl. So get your ass back here so I can finally get some rest and enjoy myself again."

"She's not my girl," John said defensively.

"You hired her."

"That doesn't make her my girl."

"I don't have time to bullshit. I've got a student with a 2.2 GPA manning the snack bar for the wrestling meet."

"Thanks for calling."

"Next Wednesday. 11:00am. Hartford Hilton."

"I don't know," John started to say before Hubbard interrupted him.

"Don't be an ass," Hubbard said just before

hanging up.

John wasn't sure how he would be received if he did show up, but he had a pretty good idea. It wasn't as if he could explain himself. That would be a bit like closing the barn door after the horses had already gotten out. And yet, he felt compelled to go, as if he had unfinished business to attend to—no matter how unpleasant it might be.

*   *   *

Alan Huber was tallish; thin--bordering on bony--with flecks of grey hair dotting his otherwise thick, dark mane, along with a confidence usually reserved for people far better looking and charismatic than he was.

"It's always a special day when we have the opportunity to recognize the wonderful accomplishments of the youth in our society," Huber began.

"This guy's kind of a tool, huh?" Hubbard whispered to Melissa as they looked on.

"And for a coach to have a part in winning two state titles in two different sports, with two different genders no less, influencing all of their lives in a positive way, is as impressive as they come..."

"But a pretty intuitive tool," Hubbard added.

"For the athletes themselves, congratulations. Your accomplishments will remain with you the rest of your lives, and will remain the envy of all you meet. Trust me on that one, as someone who never made a varsity team in high school.

Now, I know the head coach for the girls basketball team is not here today—"

"Actually, he is," John interrupted. "He's just a little late. All eyes shifted from the Governor. "And he's really sorry for that. Along with a whole host of other things."

Huber smiled. "John Mann."

John shook the hand of his one time rival. "Governor. It's been a long time."

"I see you've been quite busy," Huber laughed. "Still in demand as always."

"Well, I'm no Governor."

"I think we both know you could have been."

Not once during the ceremony or luncheon that followed did Melissa make eye contact with John. He hoped at some point to get her alone. Corner her near the bathroom. Catch her by the buffet. When it became apparent she wasn't about to let that happen, he decided a public humiliation would be the next best thing. He tapped her on the shoulder while she spoke to Huber.

"Can I speak to you a minute?" he asked.

"No," she responded flatly, barely turning around to acknowledge him.

John nodded as if he half expected that response. As a person, Melissa was as sweet as they came—until she was angry--which she was at that moment, and probably had been since the day John left without so much as a note.

"I don't blame you for being upset," he said.

"And I can't tell you how sorry I am for leaving like I did. And for not calling after and explaining why..."

She finally turned to face him.

"I changed my entire life for you. I turned down a marriage proposal for you. I threw away a seven year relationship for you. And you never even called."

A distinct and very noticeable awkwardness had settled into the room.

"I wish I could tell you I had a better reason for leaving than a bet, but I don't. I could tell you that it was about finding myself, and maybe to a certain extent it was, but it still doesn't excuse it. At the same time, it's hard for me to completely regret the things I did for one simple reason. They only served to confirm something I knew from the moment I met you—which is that wherever you are, is home for me. You—are home for me."

Tears had welled up in some of the eyes of the girls. Even Kovac seemed uncharacteristically moved. But Melissa simply left the room.

Hubbard put his arm around John. "She'll come around. You just have to give it some time."

"How much time?" John wondered.

"I'd say about five seconds," Hubbard said as she walked right back in.

What John thought might be a kiss, turned out to be a hard slap across the face instead.

"Don't ever do that again," she said. *Then*

she kissed him.

"He always did have a way with the ladies," Huber remarked.

Hubbard patted him on the back. "Don't worry, Gov, you've got yourself a pretty good gig here."

XXIV
~POST SCRIPT~

Following his fifteen minutes of fame, John turned the bar over to Abbott and I and returned to St. Francis to settle back into his life of relative obscurity. There had been talk of a movie, but when John wouldn't sell the rights unless Abbott got to play the lead, they decided to scrap the entire project. Occasionally, a reporter would call or stop by the school for a story, and John would grant every interview with the sort of speakeasy charm of someone completely comfortable with their life choices. He had already proven to himself that he was capable of doing whatever he wanted to do with his life, and that's exactly what he *was* doing.

Meanwhile, Alan Huber was re-elected Governor four years later, with an eye set towards a future run at the Presidency. He was certainly bright enough, and he wasn't a bad person. It was just ironic that Huber wasn't even the best candidate who graduated from Milford High School back in 1995.

That honor belonged to the Savior of St. Francis, The Greatest Mann in the World--the Chameleon. Of course they were all the same person, and there was a little of that person in each of us. You just had to look inside yourself to find it.

ACKNOWLEDGEMENTS

Friends have often asked me how I come up with my stories, and with the exception of a few occasions where I've had crazy dreams after eating spicy food, I have created all of my stories in the same manner. I usually start with an event or a situation that I think would be interesting. In this case, it was the idea of your average person succeeding in a high profile job if given the opportunity. Once I have the premise, I create the characters.

Are my characters based on real people? Yes and no. As I state at the beginning of this novel, it's a work of fiction, and as such, none of the characters are real. But in order to make them *appear* realistic, I try to picture what people I know might say if they found themselves in a similar situation. As a result, the characters within my stories are usually the combination of thousands of people I have met in my lifetime— people I've known for years, people I've just met, people I've worked with, people I met in passing on an airplane, or at a blackjack table in a casino.

This story is for each of you.

Enjoy this story? Turn the page for a preview glimpse at the sequel, The Greatest Mann in the World...

THE GREATEST MANN
IN THE WORLD

"Children aren't the only ones who need heroes."

Tamora Pierce

I
~SNOWIFORNIA~

What if you awoke one morning to find that everything you had known to be true and normal in your life, suddenly no longer was? What if with no advance notice whatsoever, the sun began to rise in the west and set in the east? What if on a random December day, it began snowing in Southern California and didn't stop for four months? What if at that same time, the temperature in Milford, Connecticut soared into the 80's? What if Seattle had four straight months of complete darkness followed by 20 hours a day of sunshine for three months? What if the United States was involved in a endless war that when combined with the environmental shift had caused the country to fall into a deep recession; with gas prices at an all-time high, the stock market at a 40 year low, with giant corporations going out of business on what seemed like a daily basis. What if? What if? What if?

* * * *

The day began typically enough for mid-December in the nation's capital; cold, dark and grey with a heavy fog that had settled into the district so thick that you practically had to wipe it from your

face.   People weaved their way through the
pedestrian traffic as if everyone else had been put in
front of them solely to impede them from where
they were headed. The mood in the country was as
gloomy as the weather.

Meanwhile, on the second floor conference
room in a building on the corner of 11th Street and
Pennsylvania Avenue, key members of the
Democratic National Committee were fast at work
deciding what was in the best interest of the
American people—without bothering to actually ask
them what they wanted.

It was a room filled with castoffs and wannabes.
Life for these people, with very few exceptions, had
not turned out as they had hoped when they were
younger, and they were making certain now that they
had the opportunity, to inflict payback on anyone
whose life *hadn't* been an unhappy and veritable
mess in their youth.

Dick Stoops was the unabashed leader of the
group, but certainly not for his looks or charm. He
was mostly bald, sporting the half globe, with hair on
the sides and back of his head. His voice was deep
and imposing, with the ability to drown out nearly
any sound in its path.

"Did anyone see The Post this morning?" he
asked almost rhetorically.

A woman in her late 40's, pretty beneath her red
pantsuit and white blouse, chimed in. "They're
saying that as long as we put forth a woman or a
minority as Huber's running mate, the election is
ours to lose."

"And they're right," Stoops answered. "Which is why we *will* put forth one or the other. Our job over the next several days is to talk the also-rans out of the race."

An African American man in his early 40's, who didn't seem at all bothered by their political pandering, threw in his two cents. "Do we have anything to offer them?"

"Such as?"

"Cabinet positions, future considerations...etc," the man responded.

"Jesus Christ, Ron. This isn't the NFL draft."

"I understand that, but Rick Jeremiah has plenty of money, and isn't afraid to spend it. He could drag the nomination all the way to the convention floor if he wanted to."

Stoops mulled it over for about ten seconds, which was generally the amount of time he allotted to even the most important of decisions. He hated being strong-armed into doing anything, but was also smart enough to know when to retreat.

"Ok. Tell Jeremiah he'll have a cabinet position if he withdraws and throws his support behind Huber. Tell the others to fuck off honorably or the next job they have in politics will be as a Lunch Monitor at a middle school in Poughkeepsie."

There was a noticeable chuckle in the room. It was clear that most people there loved the fact that they wielded so much power.

"What we need to figure out is who would be a better compliment to Huber. O'Bannon? Or Calvert? The African American? Or the woman? For that matter, are we sure that Huber is the person we want to put on top of the ticket? Which will play better? Thoughts?" Stoops said.

If Dan Holmes wasn't the youngest in the room, he was close to it. He looked be in his early 30's, clean-cut, well-spoken and passionate. Everything the rest of them were not. He cleared his throat before speaking, knowing full well that what he was about to say wouldn't be well received. "Isn't that for the public to decide?" he managed to spit out.

Stoops seemed more amused than annoyed. "Son, I know you're new to this game, so here's how it's played. Ninety-eight percent of the population is made up of morons who couldn't pick their nose without instructions. So it's up to us to tell them how to think based on the information we decide to leak to the press."

"Doesn't that kind of go against the very principles of a Democracy?"

There was a collective gasp in the room, followed by awkward silence, until—

"What the hell's going on out there?!" Ron exclaimed, pointing out the window for emphasis.

"The sun's out. It has happened before," Stoops answered sarcastically.

In fact, it was, having suddenly burst through the clouds like a brick thrown through a wet paper bag.

"Not just that. Why is everyone taking their jackets off?"

"They're warm?"

"When I left my house this morning, it was 12 degrees outside. They said the high was going to be

27 today."

"So the weather forecaster was wrong. That would be so shocking."

"Fifty degrees wrong?"

The people outside were wiping the sweat from their brows and looking to the heavens as if they suddenly found themselves standing beneath a giant hair dryer on the highest possible setting.

Someone slid open a window and stuck his arm out. "It's really warm. Like *really* warm," the man said.

* * * *

Three hundred miles away in Milford, Connecticut, Bernice and Joe Kreps took an unexpected stroll along the beach. They had lived in the same house directly across from the Long Island Sound for the past 37 years—which was the same length of time as their marriage. They had raised two children in that house, and seen four grandchildren walk through its doors. The house itself was a three bedroom cottage, with hardwood floors throughout and a screened in front porch, from which they spent many a night watching people walk along the beach.   *Quaint* and *comfortable* were perhaps the two most apt words used to describe the home, although their son came home one day from high school and announced that their house looked like the guesthouse to one of the million dollar estates that sandwiched it on both sides. They laughed when he said it because they knew it was true, and because they also knew they would never be able to afford to live there on an electrician and teacher's salaries if they were just starting out today. That is also what made them appreciate it as much as they did. Bernice and Joe loved taking long walks along the water and into town. They loved the little corner delis and pizza shops. And they loved that on sunny days, the light woke them up by shining brightly through the many blind free windows.

Winters had grown increasingly difficult as they grew older, and on more than one occasion, they looked into buying a second home in Florida, but simply couldn't afford it. And when December 4 began with bright, blue skies and temperatures rising through the 70's, no one appreciated it more than the Kreps.

"I mean, we're retired, so it makes sense that we're out here today," Joe told his wife while they strolled along the walking path while dozens of college age people—some wearing Yale t-shirts--played football, volleyball and Frisbee on the beach. "But what is everyone else doing out here? Don't they have school? Or jobs?"

"Not everyone thinks it's a sin to take a day off once in a while," his wife answered.

"Not taking a day off is what put two kids through college."

"You did have some help, you know."

"Yeah, but you were a teacher. Between summers and sick days, you had nearly three months off a year."

"Don't even start with me," she said.

"I'm just teasing," Joe laughed. "But I still don't

understand what all these people are doing here. That's the problem with today's society. They have no work ethic."

"You better be careful," Bernice warned, "or instead of calling you Grampy Joe, our grandchildren are going to start calling you Grumpy Joe."

Just then, three boys on bicycles whizzed past, along with two girls on roller blades, the last of which bumped Joe as she went by. "Damn teenagers," he grumbled as his wife rolled her eyes.

Across town, Professor Cummings looked out at what was supposed to be a class of forty-eight students and saw only seven. "What's the deal, ladies and gentlemen? Is it class cut day?" he asked to silence. The students that were in the room were there for a reason. They had no social skills whatsoever. It was the quietest class he ever remembered teaching.

"Tom, were you missing a lot of students today?" he asked another professor he passed on his way back to his office.

"Quite a few," was the response.

"I was missing 11 in Physics and 48 in Microbiology," Cummings lamented.

"Must be the weather. Although I'm not sure you can blame the weather for Microbiology," Tom laughed.

"But we have exams in a week, and this is *Yale*," Cummings said.

"I'm sure they'll show up as soon as the weather turns lousy again," Tom answered before adding,

"When is it going to turn back by the way?"

"I just checked it and the weather pattern shows sunny and warm the rest of the week."

"Strange pattern for December wouldn't you say? Did you hear it's snowing in Southern California?"

"It's got to be the winds of El Nino," Cummings said while shaking his head. He was easily perturbed by anything out of the norm. He was especially perturbed by anything he should understand but didn't.